ABERDEEN
CITY LIBRARIES

www.aberdeencity.gov.uk/Library
Tel: 08456 080937 or 01506 420526

Return to..
or any other Aberdeen City Library

Please return/renew this item by the last date shown
Items may also be renewed by phone or online

Published in Great Britain 2014
by Mills & Boon, an imprint of Harlequin (UK) Limited,
Eton House, 18-24 Paradise Road, Richmond, Surrey, TW9 1SR

© 2014 Christy McKellen

ISBN: 978 0 263 24224 9

Harlequin (UK) Limited's policy is to use papers that are natural, renewable and recyclable products and made from wood grown in sustainable forests. The logging and manufacturing processes conform to the legal environmental regulations of the country of origin.

Printed and bound in Great Britain
by CPI Antony Rowe, Chippenham, Wiltshire

B 000 000 011 8597

LESSONS IN RULE-BREAKING

BY
CHRISTY McKELLEN

'I'm not going to sleep with you,' she blurted before she could stop herself, her nerves riding roughshod over her common sense.

He laughed out loud, shaking his head in mirth.

'Don't worry—I'm taking a break from seducing innocent young journalists, so your virtue is safe with me,' he said, his mouth quirked in a playful smile. 'I *am* interested in your body, Jess, but only on an artistic level.'

'You can't blame me for being wary when you make provocative statements. You do have a reputation for being a bit…'

'A bit what?'

She paused, searching for the right word. 'Wild.'

He gave her a bemused grin. 'I promise to be on my best behaviour,' he said, making a crossing motion over his heart. 'And if I slip up you have my permission to *lick* me into shape.'

Oh, my *God*, the images he'd just conjured in her mind.

She really needed to get out of here before she totally lost her cool.

An overwhelming urge to pack up and go home, where she didn't have to deal with these weird and disturbing feelings he provoked in her, besieged her. But she couldn't leave. Not if she wanted to keep her job at the magazine. She was going to have to brazen it out and ignore the blatant innuendos he seemed so keen to tease her into a jittery mess with.

He was a player, all right, but she wasn't about to let him play *her*.

Dear Reader

Who can resist the dangerous charms of a bad boy? Not me! Especially a disgustingly talented one with a body built for sin and the wits to win over the hardest of women. My heroine, Jess, *is* that hard woman, and Xander, my hero, certainly has his work cut out to get the better of *her.*

These two characters were such fun to write. They're both headstrong, super-ambitious and broken in their own heart-wrenching way. Thank goodness they had me to throw them together and force them to sort out their lives!

I had the pleasure of sending them off to pass some quality time on the banks of Lake Garda—a place I have a great fondness for after spending my honeymoon there. How could they fail to fall in love in such romantic setting? I challenge anyone to resist the charms of the place.

This is a story of divine inspiration, a little bit of magic and some very messy artistic endeavours. I hope you enjoy it.

Christy x

PS I love to hear from readers. You can contact me at christymckellenauthor@gmail.com or www.facebook.com/christymckellenauthor

BK (Before Kids) **Christy McKellen** worked as a video and radio producer in London and Nottingham. After a decade of dealing with nappies, tantrums and endless questions from toddlers she has come out the other side and moved into the wonderful world of literature. She now spends her time writing flirty, sexy romance with a kick—her dream job!

In her downtime she can be found drinking the odd glass of champagne, ambling around the beautiful South West of England, or escaping from real life by dashing off to foreign lands with her fabulous family.

Christy loves to hear from readers. You can contact her at: www.christymckellen.blogspot.com, http://www.facebook.com/christymckellenauthor or https://twitter.com/ChristyMcKellen

Other Modern Tempted™ titles by Christy McKellen:

HOLIDAY WITH A STRANGER

This and other titles by Christy McKellen are available as eBooks from www.millsandboon.co.uk

To the Prosecco Book Club ladies
for their encouragement and friendship.

And to Clio, my fantastic editor,
thanks for your positivity and unerring support.

CHAPTER ONE

'The editor wants to see you in her office.'

Jessica LaFayette glanced up from the screen of her laptop to see Claire, one of the other junior staff writers at *Spark* magazine, looking down at her with worry in her eyes and a speculative eyebrow raised.

Clearly Claire was as concerned as Jess about what sort of news was about to be bestowed on her.

There had been rumours flying about the office recently about staff cutbacks and everyone had been on tenterhooks for weeks, desperately worried that they were the one about to be summoned to the editor's office in order to be given the boot.

Okay, time to buckle up.

Smoothing a hand down her hair and straightening her blouse, Jess gave Claire a curt nod and stood up, balling her trembling hands into fists at her sides, before striding over to the editor's office.

If she lost this job she was in big trouble. She'd already raced through her meagre savings living in London as an intern for nine months, before finally securing the job here—on the proviso she made it past her three-month probation period. The thought of having to pack up and go home to live back with her parents in the burbs of Leicester, after all the excitement of finally being employed in her dream job, sent a twist of panic through her.

They thought she was crazy chasing such a competitive career, but it was what she'd always wanted to do and she'd been determined to give it everything she had.

She was stubborn like that.

It had taken her two years after leaving university to land a placement at *Spark*, two long years of living back at home with a woman who would surely place as a top contender for 'World's Most Disappointed Mother.'

Jess was *not* the daughter Ingrid LaFayette had hoped for. Instead of a vivacious, beauty—a carbon copy of herself—she'd been lumped with kooky-looking, strong-willed Jess.

No way was she going back to the raised eyebrows and tense silences that she'd lived with for longer than she wanted to remember. Life had moved on and so had she.

Pushing back her shoulders and taking a deep breath, Jess rapped on the glass partition of her editor's office before walking in.

Pamela Bradley—editor extraordinaire—looked up from her computer and waved Jess into the office with a perfectly manicured hand.

All the women who worked on the magazine rocked up to work every day looking as if they'd just stepped off a Paris catwalk—all except for Jess. She preferred to stick with her smart, comfortably fitting suits. She knew her limitations when it came to fashion—she hadn't a clue what was supposed to suit her body shape and didn't want to make a fool of herself by looking as if she was trying too hard. She was a smart, but practical, girl through and through.

'Jess, sit.' Pamela gestured towards the chair facing

her and Jess sat down on the edge of the seat, her hands folded neatly in her lap, and waited, her heart thumping hard against her chest.

'So, I read your piece on nail salons.' Pamela gave her a steely-eyed look and Jess shrank back into her seat under the confidence-wrecking force of it.

Uh-oh. That wasn't the look of unadulterated joy and respect she'd been hoping for.

'To be perfectly honest, Jess, it wasn't good enough. The pieces you've been submitting recently have been a little… How can I put this?' She put both hands onto the desk in front of her, her nails digging into the wood like talons, and leant forward. 'Dry. Lifeless. Dull.' The words snapped out of her mouth as if she found them utterly distasteful. She gave a small shake of her perfectly coiffed head. 'I expected more, Jess, when I offered you the position here.'

Fear and embarrassment wound through Jess's chest and pooled like burning acid in her stomach.

She'd blown it. Pamela had to make someone redundant and it looked as if it was going to be her head on the block.

'I c-can do better,' she stuttered out, desperate to stall the words she felt sure were about to trip from Pamela's lips.

Pamela shook her head and her mouth twisted into a dissatisfied smile. 'I gave you the job because I sensed there was some hidden potential there, Jess. You're a talented writer, methodical with an accomplished style, but your writing lacks the edge you need to make your pieces really stand out. It's *too* controlled, too stuffy.'

'I can unstuff it,' Jess yelped, feeling tears of frustration burning at the backs of her eyes.

'How do you propose to do that, Jess?'

Jess mouthed at her, totally at a loss for how to answer.

'To be frank, I think you need to stop living in that self-controlled little bubble,' Pamela continued, eyeing the immaculate, but understated, suit Jess was wearing today.

Jess smoothed her skirt down, then her hair. 'I don't understand what you mean.'

'Look, Jess, I think you're a talented writer and you could build a great career with us here, but my advice to you is that you need to find that extra something to make your work sparkle. To find the life beyond your neat little world.' She tipped her head in a motherly sort of way. 'When did you last go out on a date, for example?'

The question made Jess uneasy. 'What does that have to do with anything?'

'You're what? Twenty-five? You take life too seriously. You should be out, having wild sex and falling in love at your age. Widening your experiences.'

'Sex is overrated,' Jess muttered, thinking back to the awkward sexual experiences she'd had up till this point. She didn't get what all the fuss was about when it came to sex. It was uncomfortable and messy and she was usually glad when it was all over if she was totally honest. Neither of the guys she'd slept with had rocked her world, but at the time she'd thought she ought to put the effort in, just to see what she was supposedly missing out on.

It turned out she wasn't missing much at all.

There was a knock on the partition behind her and Jess turned to see Pamela's assistant standing there with a slip of paper clutched in her hand.

'Sorry to interrupt, but Maggie just phoned. She's stuck in Greece because of an air-traffic-controllers strike and can't make it back for her assignment today. She sounded pretty fed up because apparently she'd managed to snag an interview with Xander Heaton, that bad-boy artist everyone's so crazy about.'

Pamela sighed. 'Can't she reschedule? I really need that piece in the next issue. Xander was going to be the linchpin of the article.'

'Apparently not. He's refusing to change the date because he's about to start working on a new exhibition. He'll be at his studio in Old Street today, but he's off to Italy tonight and he never gives any press interviews while he's working. Something about killing his muse.'

'Yeah, okay.' Pamela sighed, flapping a hand in a tired manner. 'Can Marnie go?' she asked, clearly not that hopeful.

'She's off with the flu. Nearly half the office has called in sick this week.'

'I can go and cover it,' Jess said a little too loudly, her heart racing as a sudden shot of adrenaline fired round her body. If she didn't grab this opportunity quickly one of the other junior writers would and she really needed to show Pamela some of that spark she was so keen to see.

'I don't know, Jess.' Pamela flipped her a look of deep scepticism.

'Please, Pam, give me another chance to show you how I can make my writing sizzle.' Jess leant forward in her chair, clasping her hands together in a prayer of hope. 'It would be such a shame to miss out on the opportunity of interviewing him while he's in the country.'

'You think you're up to handling someone like Xander Heaton, do you?'

Jess sat up straighter, pulled taut by a thread of hope. 'Of course I am. How difficult can he be?'

She could have sworn she saw an amused smirk flit across Pamela's face.

'Okay, then,' Pamela said, finally. 'If he's working with a model, make sure you talk to her, too, if you get the opportunity—see if you can get something interesting. What he's like to work with, whether she's sleeping with him, why he picked her as his model, anything to give the piece an edge. Try and get a sense of who he is, any personal details you can draw out of him. He's got himself a reputation as a real playboy over the last year—he's turned up to pretty much every high-profile party going and caused a scene at all of them—so see if you can get some gossip about what happened there. Oh, and try and find out why he hasn't produced anything of note recently, too. His last exhibition was a real critical flop so that might have something to do with it. And most importantly, find out what he's planning to do for his next project.'

Jess was nodding so much her neck was starting to ache. 'Okay, got it. No problem.' She stood up and smiled at Pamela. 'Thank you, for giving me another chance.'

Pamela raised a severely plucked eyebrow. 'Don't waste this opportunity, Jess. If you want to keep your job on this magazine you're going to have to pull something pretty special out of the bag.'

Pamela's words rang in Jess's ears as she took the tube over to Old Street.

She made copious notes on the way, determined to remember everything Pamela had asked for.

The train had just reached Moorgate station when it slowed down to a crawl, then stopped, midjourney.

The driver's voice came over the tannoy to let the passengers know there was an electrical fault with the train, but they were hoping to get it sorted out in a few minutes.

Jess looked about her wildly; she was already running late to hit the allotted time for her interview with Xander and she didn't want to turn up there flustered and on the back foot. She wanted him to be impressed with her cool professionalism and trust her enough to spill the sort of information she needed to make her piece stand out from the ones he'd done in the past.

She'd seen pictures of him in the press—at parties with the great and good of London society, usually with some eminently beautiful woman hanging off his arm— and she knew in her bones he was going to be a challenge. If she was going to win him over she couldn't allow herself to be daunted by that famous dark charisma and overabundance of sexual confidence.

He was exactly the sort of man she usually avoided in real life. Bad-boy types who flitted from woman to woman like moths in a lighting shop were the antithesis of what she was looking for in a partner. She needed steady and safe. Comfortable. A relationship she could feel in control of.

A nervous shiver tickled down her spine at the thought of facing him, but she shook it off. She was *not* going to let his challenging reputation get to her. She was a smart, savvy, professional woman and that was exactly what he was going to see—when she finally arrived there.

She sat there for another fifteen minutes, tapping her feet and biting at a ragged fingernail until the train finally began its excruciatingly slow roll into Old Street station.

She was now officially late for her interview.

She hated being late. Hated it.

Anything that took control out of her hands like this made her so stressed she felt ill with it.

After a few more frustrating minutes of trying to figure out where she was meant to be going using the sat nav on her phone, she finally found the converted warehouse where Xander's studio was located.

Feeling sticky and jumpy after running all the way there in her heels, she stepped into the blissfully cool entrance lobby and looked at the list of names and businesses on the large brushed-metal sign. Xander's studio was just one of a collection of spaces used by a group of high-profile artists and creatives.

The place was shabby chic through and through with huge, squashy leather sofas scattered around a break-out kitchen area, all done out in stainless steel and black lacquer-fronted cupboards. Amazing murals had been painted on all the walls and Jess recognised one in Xander's famously biting style. It was a social commentary on the state of reporting in the press. An open newspaper showed a picture of a child crying, with a meat cleaver slicing through the middle of it and the word *HACK* painted in big red bloody letters along the blade.

Okay, she really needed to stop looking at that before *the fear* got to her. Did he really hate journalists that much? Would that make it even harder for her to conduct a successful interview with him?

Only one way to find out.

Gritting her teeth and smoothing down the jacket of her suit, she walked up the stairs to where Xander's studio was located on the third floor.

Taking a moment to get her breath back, she knocked

loudly on the heavy wooden door to his studio and stood back to wait for him to appear, her hands grasped tightly behind her back and what she hoped was an open and friendly smile plastered across her face.

There was the sound of footsteps from the other side of the door and Jess steeled herself as it swung open to reveal Xander Heaton, with a paintbrush in one hand and a look of tense annoyance on his face.

Jess couldn't help but stand and stare up at him as he towered over her. She'd anticipated him being somehow disappointing in the flesh, but he wasn't. He *really* wasn't.

Paint-splattered jeans hung low on his hips and a grey cotton T-shirt clung tightly to the hard contours of his chest, making no effort whatsoever to disguise the swell of muscles on his rangy frame.

Despite the hard angles of his bone structure there was something faintly boyish about him. Perhaps that was the key to his appeal? A hard alpha male on the outside with just a glimmer of a softer, more vulnerable soul inside.

There was an almost ethereal glow about him, too, as if his charisma were being overmanufactured inside his body and the excess were spilling out through the pores of his skin.

Even his just-rolled-out-of-bed, designer mess of rich chestnut-brown hair seemed to glow like a freshly shelled conker in the sunshine pouring in through the large warehouse windows.

Jess's body buzzed with longing to reach up and run her hands over his face, to feel the hard contours of his bones under that golden skin and the gentle rasp of his barely there stubble as it caught on the whorls of her fingertips.

It took her a moment to realise he was staring at her mouth with his amazing, bright, aqua-coloured eyes and giving her an impatient frown as if he was utterly nonplussed by her appearance and thoroughly pissed off about being disturbed.

She gave herself a little shake and pulled herself together. She was a twenty-five-year-old professional woman, not some love-struck teenager, and she needed to act like it.

'Hi, Xander, I'm here to do the interview with you today,' she said brightly. 'Maggie's caught up so you've got me instead.' Her smile began to falter when he didn't give up his hard frown. 'I know I'm a few minutes late, but it was totally beyond my control. The tube train I was on…' She ground to a halt as he began shaking his head.

'I have no idea what you're talking about.'

Panic rose in her chest and her blood began pumping round her body with such vigorous force she could feel the jittery buzz of it right down to her toes. 'The interview. With Maggie? She said you'd agreed to talk to her today about the new exhibition you're planning.' He continued to stare at her blankly. 'Before you go to Italy,' Jess said, gesticulating wildly now, as if she could somehow waft the memory of the interview back into his head through the sheer force of her determination.

Her rambling explanation must have sparked something in his brain because his eyes widened a fraction before his expression shut down into a hard frown again.

'Yeah, okay, I'd forgotten about that…' he shrugged '…but you missed your window. I'm right in the middle of something now.'

'But…' Jess could barely get the words past her lips in her panic.

'Sorry, sweetheart, but you snooze, you lose.' He turned to go.

'What? That's it? You can't even give me five minutes of your time?' she nearly shouted in her panic.

Xander sighed and turned back, rubbing a hand through his hair. 'To be honest, I never wanted to do this interview in the first place. I only agreed because your colleague is a friend of a friend and she caught me at a weak moment. I seem to remember I was pretty drunk.' He leant against the doorjamb and flashed her a 'crap happens' look. 'I don't have time to pander to journalists right now. I have work to do. Now, if you'll excuse me.' He shot her a wink before striding off into his studio, slamming the door behind him and leaving Jess mouthing like a landed fish in his wake.

Xander Heaton walked back to where he'd been sketching his model, trying to shake off an unsettling twinge of guilt as the look of utter dismay on the journalist's face permeated through to his conscience.

He flipped it out of his head. He didn't need distractions like that at the moment. It was hard enough holding it together without having to accommodate any old Tom, Dick or Harriet who wandered in for a bit of show-and-tell. Everyone seemed to want a piece of him at the moment and he barely had enough of himself left to keep his strung-out existence going.

His latest model—who was giving it everything she'd got to contort herself into the strange pose he'd asked her to take up—gave him a slow, seductive smile as he sat down and attempted to focus back on her.

Ah, hell. He knew he'd been playing with fire when he asked her to pose for a picture. She'd been one of a bunch of professional models he'd got talking to at a party and he'd thought she might be an interesting subject to paint. She was making it pretty clear she was interested in more than just modelling for him right now, though.

She was a beautiful woman—too young for his tastes—but she was going to be a big thing at some point, he could tell. He should be excited about working with her, but somehow he couldn't summon the energy for it today.

A wave of tiredness crashed over him. He'd been searching for inspiration for this new exhibition for months, desperately trying to drop-kick his muse into action, but for some reason he kept missing his mark. He'd ended up destroying every picture he'd painted recently, disgusted by the banal rubbish he was coming up with. Just like the picture he'd been working on before he was interrupted.

The dark-haired journalist's face slid back into his mind as he tore off the page in the sketchbook he'd been working on, crumpled it up and lobbed it at the bin.

She had enormous eyes, he reflected now, dark blue with bright, white flecks that had drawn him right in. She wasn't conventionally attractive, but there'd been a kind of spirit about her that had made his blood pump faster. Thinking back, there had been something about her expression that disturbed him when he'd said *no* to the interview. It hadn't been the usual sort of annoyance or disappointment he tended to invoke in journos when he refused to talk to them—she'd looked as if he'd just stomped hard on her life's dream and left it broken and bleeding on the floor.

He had a sudden mad urge to sketch the image that had just pinged into his head. It was brighter and clearer and sharper than anything he'd envisaged in a very long time and his sluggish blood picked up speed as a long-forgotten feeling of elation coursed through him.

Rubbing his hand over his eyes, he felt the puffiness that had taken up residence there since the insomnia had set in. It had been months since he'd slept properly and no matter what he tried it wouldn't break its hold on him.

It appeared to be making him crazy.

'Everything okay, Xander?' his model, Seraphina, asked, unfolding herself from the chair and sauntering over to where he sat with his now blank sketch pad on his knee. 'Hmm, so are you using invisible ink here, or what?' she asked.

He flashed her a look of irritation and her smile faltered.

Guilt pulled at him and he replaced the unreasonable expression with an apologetic smile to try and make up for offending her. 'Look, Sera, I'm sorry but this isn't working out.'

'What? I'm not making your creative juices flow? Do you need a bit of inspiration?' she asked, her voice laden with innuendo.

Before he could react she slipped her top over her head, stepped close and picked up his hand, pressing it to her bare breast.

He felt nothing.

Closing his eyes, he shook his head and carefully removed his hand.

He'd partied hard this year, needing an outlet for his frustration and anger after the cutting reviews of his last exhibition—where the reviewers had wondered in

full public view where his talent had disappeared to—
but it had all caught up with him recently.

He felt hollowed out by all the vacuous affairs with
an ever-changing kaleidoscope of willing women, none
of whom lasted for more than a couple of months. He'd
been constantly on the lookout for something new and
fresh and revitalising to draw him out of his depressed
funk but he'd overindulged, leaving him feeling strung
out and empty.

His work had suffered. Big time. In fact he couldn't
remember the last time he'd felt a genuine urge to pick
up a paintbrush, or pencils, or even a spray can and
make his mark. He felt washed up, wrung out and des-
iccated.

Looking up at Seraphina, he was horrified to see
tears had welled in her eyes. He held up a placating
hand—none of this was her fault and he felt a sting of
shame at hurting her. 'Look, you're a beautiful woman,
but you're not what I need right now.'

'What *do* you need?'

'I don't know, Sera. I wish I did. I'll know it when
I see it.'

'Fine,' she interjected, her voice wobbly and high. 'If
I'm not good enough for you I'm not wasting my time
hanging around here.' Pulling her top back on, she gave
him one last accusatory look before storming out, slamming the door behind her.

Jess was smoothing her hair down with a shaking hand
and trying to pull herself together in the loos across
from Xander's studio when the door flew open and a
tall, beautiful woman stormed in and slumped against
the porcelain washbasin, swiping away a waterfall of

tears that were making her meticulously applied make-up run.

'Are you okay?' Jess asked, grateful for a reprieve from worrying about her own problems for a moment. She wondered whether the woman was anything to do with Xander. She wouldn't be at all surprised.

The woman glanced up into the mirror. 'I'm fine,' she said, giving a shaky smile before looking away again.

Jess went into the toilet to grab some tissue and placed it on the basin next to the woman before leaning back against the wall in companionable silence. The woman nodded in surprised thanks and picked up the tissue, dabbing under her eyes.

She was incredible-looking, all Bambi limbs and delicate bone structure. Her huge blue eyes seemed to glow with life—even through the tears—and her skin... What Jess wouldn't give for flawless, soft skin like hers.

She pulled her long suit jacket around her, feeling like a massive frumpy lump in comparison.

'Are you sure you're okay?' Jess asked.

'Yeah. Feeling humiliated and rejected, but I'll survive.'

Jess snorted. 'Join the club.'

The woman looked at her in confusion. 'What happened to you?'

Jess sighed. 'I was supposed to be interviewing Xander Heaton but he blew me off.'

The woman snorted. 'Sounds like Xander. Does what he wants, when he feels like it and sod everyone else. He's a law unto himself, that guy.'

Aha, so she was right.

'What did he do to make you cry?' Jess asked tentatively. If she couldn't get an interview with the man himself, she could at least get some information from one of his disgruntled models to try and appease Pamela.

The model looked down at the sink. 'I've been stupidly excited about working with him and I've been telling everyone I'm going to be in a famous painting, but apparently I'm totally uninspiring. He doesn't think I'm attractive enough,' she said quietly. 'He was all sweetness one minute and cold as ice the next and I have no idea what I did wrong.'

A shot of anger fired through Jess's veins. Just who did the guy think he was? 'What's your name?' Jess asked gently.

'Seraphina.'

'Well, I think you're a very beautiful woman and Xander's an idiot to reject you,' Jess said, giving the woman an encouraging smile. 'From what I've heard about him you've had a lucky escape. He's not exactly known for having meaningful relationships.'

The model snorted, but managed to raise a smile. 'No, I guess not. And it's not as if he made a move on me, but I hoped he might.' She looked down at the floor. 'I just got a bit swept away by the excitement of it all and he's *so* damn hot. You can't blame a girl for falling for him.'

Jess nodded. Okay, well, that answered the *'are you sleeping with him?'* question. 'Yeah, I imagine that's easily done.' She brushed a speck of dust off the sleeve of her jacket. 'Right, well, I'd better go. I have to go back to work and persuade my editor not to fire me.'

Her stomach sank at the thought of returning and admitting she'd failed.

Seraphina gave Jess a sympathetic smile. 'Good luck.'

'You, too,' Jess said, giving the girl's arm a reassuring squeeze before leaving her alone in the bathroom—hot wrath at Xander rising like an out-of-control soufflé in her chest.

Xander was locking up the studio when the dark-haired journalist slammed through the ladies' toilet door and stalked towards him. Her cheeks were flushed and disdain and anger flashed in those huge midnight-blue eyes of hers.

She jerked to a halt, a dark frown marring her face, before turning to go on her way. She'd only taken two steps before she swivelled back to face him again. 'What the hell is wrong with you?' she practically spat.

He took a step backwards in surprise. 'What are you talking about?'

'The way you treated that woman is inhumane.'

He frowned at her hard, baffled. 'What woman?'

She threw her hands up in disgust. 'Seraphina.'

Her reprimanding tone bothered him. Who was she to tell him how to conduct himself? 'She needs to toughen up if she's going to make it as a model.'

Her eyes widened in contemptuous disbelief. 'Not everyone has rhino skin. Can't you remember what it feels like to be young and filled with hope and excitement for the future?'

There was a hint of expectation in her face, as if she wanted to hear him admit to his weaknesses out loud.

His automatic privacy barriers shot up.

Not a chance, journo.

'I don't think I've ever been filled with hope. I may have *filled* a Hope in my time, though.' He flashed her a grin and took a step towards her.

Her frown deepened and she took a shaky step away. 'Have you always been this arrogant?'

He grinned. He couldn't help it. It was too tempting not to tease her, to see that passion flash in those amazing eyes again. 'Yes.'

Shaking her head, she looked away from him, over his shoulder at the closed studio door. 'No wonder everyone's beginning to think you're just some washed-up playboy. I'm not surprised your reputation's on the rocks if that's the way you treat people.'

Indignation trickled through him. That was a low blow. He couldn't let her get to him, though; she had no idea what it was like living in his world. Perhaps she wouldn't be quite so quick to judge if she did.

The immense pressure to continually produce better and better work had been a killer to his self-confidence, and more importantly to his self-control when it came to distractions.

Not that he was about to explain that to her.

She turned back to face him and he stared into her eyes for a moment, lost in their depths. Her little show of snappy rebellion intrigued him—in more ways than one.

She was properly saucy, in a hands-off-the-merchandise kind of way. Her face wasn't classically beautiful: her nose was a little too big, her eyes set too far apart, but there was definitely something striking about her. He was pretty sure there was more going on behind that guarded expression, too, that wasn't quite reaching surface level. The suit that hung so badly on her curvy frame looked like something a fifty-year-old woman might choose to wear and the long bob of dark hair she sported dragged her already long face down. She was all buttoned up—her youth and vitality clearly being repressed and controlled.

The thought of getting beneath that well-secured facade made him want things. Things he really shouldn't be wanting right then, not when he ought to be swearing off women until he started producing some decent art for this long-overdue exhibition.

His gaze dropped to her small, cupid-lipped mouth and he wondered for a second what it would feel like to kiss her, how she would taste on his tongue, before dismissing the idea. He *really* needed to focus right now.

A flash of him sitting down to capture this intriguing contradiction of a woman in paint and pencils flitted through his head. He'd love to have her pose for him. He hadn't felt this captivated by anyone or anything for such a long time it was as if he'd been given a shot of adrenaline to the heart. His fingers itched to pick up his pencil and start sketching her face.

She threw her hands up in exasperation when he failed to respond to her last jibe. 'Okay, well, I guess I'd better leave you and your *massive ego* in peace so you can get back to work.'

Turning on her heel, she strode away from him, her shoulders pulled forward with tension and her hands balled at her sides.

'Let me draw you.' The words came out of his mouth before she reached the stairwell, stopping her abruptly in her tracks.

She turned round to face him and her look of utter confusion made him laugh out loud. She'd make a great comic actor.

'What did you say?' The words seemed to catch in her throat and she gave a little cough at the end as if to clear the blockage.

He walked over to where she was standing. 'I'm in

need of a portrait model and I think you'd make a fascinating subject.'

'You want *me* to pose for you?'

'Sure, why not?'

'Firstly, because I have a job as a serious *journalist*, and secondly, because I've seen how you treat your models and, I have to say, I'm not champing at the bit to get the same treatment.'

He startled her by lifting a hand and running it vigorously over his face before snorting with laughter. 'Okay, *Lois Lane*, but in my defence Sera was the one up for more than just modelling and I was being a gentleman for once by turning her down,' he said, resting one arm against the wall behind her so it nearly touched her shoulders. 'That's why she was so mad at me.'

She seemed to bristle at his close proximity and readjusted her stance to lean away from him. He tried hard not to let her casual rebuttal bother him.

'Okay, clearly I'm off my game and I apologise for being rude to you earlier,' he said, tipping his head to one side in an attempt to mollify her. 'Can we call a truce and start again?'

He stared at her hard, attempting to commit her face to memory in case she refused his offer and he never saw her again. The thought bothered him more than it should considering they'd only just met. What was it about her that he found so enticing?

'Okay. Truce,' she agreed, smoothing her hand down the front of her immaculate blouse.

'How about this?' he suggested, spurred on by her acceptance. 'You come out to Italy for a few days and let me draw you and I'll give you an exclusive interview.'

Her eyes widened at the—admittedly rather out of

the blue—offer. 'You want me to go all the way to Italy to interview you? Why can't we do it here, now?'

'Because I need to leave for the airport in a couple of hours and I want to be able to give you my full attention. It's Italy or bust.' He had to forcibly stop himself from dropping his gaze to her own rather impressive bust that nestled beneath her shapeless, overlarge jacket. He didn't want her to think he was asking her to do more than pose for him. He didn't need a complication like that right now, not when he'd finally started to feel the buzz of creativity that had been eluding him for so long.

She stared at him for another minute, clearly trying to process it all, twisting her hands together as she thought about it.

'What's the matter, Miss Prim, too wild for you? Perhaps I should offer an exclusive to one of your rivals instead. I'm sure it would help sell a truckload of *their* magazines.'

Her eyes widened at the challenge and he wondered for a moment whether she'd be brave enough to rise to it. He sensed from her earlier frustration that she was hungry for an interview with him, so perhaps this would push her to say yes.

He hoped so. He really wanted her to come now he'd suggested it.

She was twisting her fingers together as she thought about it, but when she caught him looking at her hands she crossed her arms defensively in front of her. 'Okay. I'll come to Italy and sit for a portrait, but I want an in-depth interview, not just the usual pat answers you reel out for everyone else.'

He raised an eyebrow. There was no way he was giving her anything *deeply* private, but he could break his no-discussing-anything-personal rule just this once. It would be worth it if it meant finally breaking his dry spell and getting this exhibition off the ground.

'Deal.' He went back into the studio and jotted down the address of the villa on the banks of Lake Garda, which he was borrowing from a friend for a few weeks while he worked on his exhibition in peace and isolation. A complete change of scene was exactly what he needed right now in order to get his head straight. He felt stifled here in London. He needed space and sunshine and fresh air.

Coming back out, he handed her the slip of paper and she took it with a shaking hand. Was she nervous? The idea of it surprised him. She seemed so put-together with her straight clothes and strident manner.

'Maybe we should formally introduce ourselves,' he said, flipping her a cheeky grin and smiling as a pink hue tipped her cheekbones. 'Xander Heaton.' He extended a hand and she put her own small, cold one into it. Her grip was firm, though, which surprised him. Usually women did that limp-handed press that left him feeling as if he were an overzealous brute when he shook hands with them.

'Jessica LaFayette. My friends call me Jess,' she said, giving him a tight smile.

He grinned. 'So which should I use? Clearly I haven't made it into the friends bracket yet.'

'Jess is fine,' she said. 'But I might withdraw the privilege if you do something else to annoy me.' She flashed him a more relaxed smile this time, a hint of playfulness flashing in her eyes.

He laughed at that. 'You have cold hands, Jess,' he said, enclosing hers in both of his.

'But a warm heart,' she said, giving him a solicitous smile before pulling her hands firmly out of his grip.

She was going to be a fascinating subject to get to the heart of. The mere thought of it excited him. She was exactly the breath of fresh air he needed.

He was finally on his way back to the big time, baby.

CHAPTER TWO

TWENTY-FOUR HOURS later Jess stared out of the windscreen of her hire car in wonder as the incredible scenery around Lake Garda flew by.

Pamela had been bemused at first by Jess's assertions that she would get a great exclusive out of Xander if she followed him all the way to Italy for the interview, but in the end she'd agreed to let Jess go if she stumped up for the flight and accommodation herself. She was also to visit some of the towns that bordered the lake and write some short 'Best Places to Holiday in Northern Italy' pieces for the travel section while she was there. The magazine didn't have the resources to send their staffers off to 'just swan around the Italian Lakes,' or so Pamela claimed.

Jess had taken it on the chin and booked herself onto the cheapest flight she could find the next day and found a room in a rather dubious-looking two-star hotel, which was the only place available on Lake Garda at short notice that didn't cost more per day than the rent on her flat for the entire month.

The memory of Xander's challenging look when he'd asked her to come to Italy made her insides twist and swoop. In that moment before responding, she'd thought about what Pamela had said about how she needed to live a little to become a better writer, and how much she wanted to keep her hard-fought-for job at the magazine, and despite hating the idea of sitting for a picture for him—frankly it was her idea of hell to be scrutinised from all angles by a man who made her feel so unsettled—she found herself agreeing to it if it meant he'd give her what she wanted. Strike that, what she *needed*.

No way was she going to let this once-in-a-lifetime opportunity slip away from her.

Before she'd left, Pam had pulled her to one side and reminded her that Xander was notoriously difficult to interview and that she should try and stay objective. She didn't say the words, 'Don't let him twist you round his finger and into his bed', but they were very much implied.

Jess had smiled to herself; as if *that* were ever likely to happen. Flings were not her thing and definitely *not* with men like Xander.

She had more sense than that.

As the villa where Xander was staying swung into view she took a deep breath to quell a disorientating surge of jittery excitement as she took in the sight of immaculately landscaped gardens and the imposing seventeenth-century building that resided like a noble queen over spectacular views of Lake Garda.

She'd never seen anything so perfectly picturesque in her life.

She could barely believe she was here to spend a couple of days hanging out with Xander Heaton, disgustingly talented artist, womaniser and undisputable contender for sexiest man alive.

Glancing down at the neat, but unfussy, trouser suit she'd put on for travelling, she acknowledged with a sinking feeling that she was *not* going to feel comfortable in his world.

Still, she was determined to make the most of the time she had with him. She just needed to hold her nerve and not let him intimidate her.

Ah, hell, who was she kidding? She was going to be a wreck from beginning to end. The trick was not to let him see it.

She drove up to the front of a long sweep of sandy-coloured stone steps and parked up. Swinging the door open, she got out and stretched her back, which ached like hell after being cramped up for hours, first on the plane, then in the car as she'd swung it through the Italian countryside.

Looking up at the magnificence of the building, she felt another sting of insignificance.

Get it together, Jess, you have nothing to feel humbled about.

The door to the villa opened and a handsome middle-aged woman in a beautifully cut shift dress appeared. Her long swathe of dark hair swung across her back as she walked down the steps towards where Jess was standing.

'Ms LaFayette?' she asked, holding out a welcoming hand.

Jess shook it. 'Call me Jess,' she said, giving the woman a friendly smile back.

'I'm Rosa. I'm the housekeeper here. If you need anything during your stay please let me know.'

Jess stared at her, confused. 'Oh, I'm not staying here. I've booked a room in a hotel down the road. The Royal, I think it's called.'

Rosa frowned, looking flustered. 'Oh, my mistake. Well, I hope they give you a good room there.' The uncertainty in Rosa's voice made something pinch in Jess's chest. Did The Royal have a bad reputation?

Ah, whatever. She was only going to be staying for two nights, so it wouldn't matter, and it was all she could afford anyway. This wasn't a holiday, she reminded herself, it was an assignment. The first of many more, she hoped—once she'd blown Pamela away with her fun, but insightful, piece on Xander.

Another thought struck her. Had Xander given the impression she was here for more than just business? Or had Rosa just assumed she was because of his track record?

Shaking off the unnerving tingle deep in her pelvis at the thought of getting up close and personal with Xander, she smoothed down a wrinkle in the sleeve of her jacket with shaking fingers. She should really take the thing off, it was already making her hot in the intense heat of the afternoon, but she wanted to stay formal and professional to remind him she was here as a serious journalist and not someone to be toyed with. There would be no flirting and manipulating the situation by Xander.

Control, Jess, cool, calm control.

'Is Xander around?' Jess asked, determined to get this interview under way as soon as possible. Pamela had only given her a week to get the article written. They were going with a *Great Artists of the Twenty-First Century* theme and Xander's interview was going to be the showcase piece, so it had to be good. If she didn't manage to produce something whiz-bang enough Pam had suggested she'd have to pass on Jess's notes to Maggie and have her write the article instead.

No *way* was Jess going to let that happen. This was

her big opportunity to prove to Pamela she was the right fit for *Spark*.

She just needed to get Xander to trust her enough to open up and talk.

Rosa nodded. 'He's down at the villa's private beach. Just follow the path over there to the lake.' She pointed in the direction she meant.

Jess thanked her and set off to the beach, pulling the hem of her blouse down where it had ridden up over her middle and swiping a rather damp hand over her hair.

The path took her through a small grove of sweet-smelling olive trees and opened up onto a small, sandy cove with spectacular views across to the other side of the lake.

There was no sign of Xander at first, but as she looked around she noticed a movement in the clear, still water of the lake.

Jess came to an abrupt halt as Xander stood up from where he'd been swimming, gleaming rivulets of water running down from his hair and cascading over his naked chest. She watched, mesmerised, as he waded towards her, his movements agile and smooth as he powered through the water.

He glanced up and saw her standing there, tipping her a mischievous grin and giving her a welcoming salute.

'Jess, good to see you.'

She watched him advance towards her, rooted to the spot and with an unnerving pulse beating in her throat.

His golden skin gleamed in the bright afternoon light, the gentle rays highlighting every contour of his solid frame, and as he pushed his wet hair back from his angular face, making the muscles of his chest twist and flex, she had to suppress a squeak of pure delight.

There was unbridled power in his stride, as he quickly covered the ground between them, that made her insides jump and twist with pleasure.

Scuffing her toes into the sand, she gave herself a lecture on the evils of letting her overactive imagination get the better of her.

'Hey,' Xander said, when he finally reached her, flashing her a grin that made her stomach lurch with lust. Drops of water clung to his eyelashes, making them look obscenely long and lush as they framed those incredible eyes of his.

Jess swallowed, trying to loosen up her throat, which was tight with tension. Shaking her nerves off before they took too firm a hold, she reminded herself that she was here to work, and that was what she was damn well going to do.

'H-hello. This place is beautiful,' she managed to stutter out, cursing the shake in her voice. She was having immense trouble keeping her gaze on his face and not allowing it to drop to the incredible physique of his chest.

'It's a friend's holiday home. Pretty impressive, huh?'

'Yup. Impressive.' It seemed she was totally out of intelligent conversation. Not a great start for someone who was supposed to be a wordsmith for a living.

'I'm heading back up to the villa for tea and cake. Rosa makes the best summer panettone. Come and join me.' It wasn't a question and she bristled a little at his bossy tone.

'I'm not hungry. I had a late lunch.'

He gave her a slow, sexually laden smile that made her stomach swoop alarmingly. 'Well, I'm hungry.'

The gentle breeze caught her hair and blew it across her suddenly incredibly hot face. Before she could react, he took a step towards her, lifted his hand and slid his long fingers against her cheek, then tucked the rogue curl of hair behind her ear. It was such an intimate thing to do she was utterly lost for words, and, instead of speaking, she found herself staring at his mouth, totally transfixed by the fullness of his lips as they parted slightly, revealing his perfect white teeth. The heat of his almost naked body bled into her skin and she took a deep, calming breath in, only to draw the musky fragrance of his skin into her nostrils, sending her senses spinning out of control.

Every bit of her body felt energised and tingly—the anticipation of what could happen if he just leant forward a couple of inches burning like wildfire in her chest. Was he going to…?

Kiss me.

She wasn't sure for a second whether she'd said it out loud and she skimmed her gaze up to look into his eyes, hoping desperately it had only been an errant voice in her head.

His gaze flicked between her eyes, the bright aqua of his irises captivating her with their other-worldliness.

What the hell was going on here? A nervy panic rose inside her, causing a wave of jittery heat to rush up her neck. She couldn't handle this. Not here, in broad daylight, totally unprepared for what might happen if he kept on looking at her like that.

Xander must have sensed her panic because he took a step away from her, giving her the space and air she suddenly craved.

'You okay, Jess?' he said, bemused concern clear in his voice.

'Fine. I'm fine,' she managed to gasp, forcing a smile onto her face. 'Just a bit hot in the sun.' She flapped a hand in front of her face in a pathetic attempt to cool herself down. 'I have to go and check in to my hotel but I wanted to let you know I'd arrived. I'd like to make a plan for starting the interview so we can get started as soon as possible.' She kept her voice clipped and businesslike, trying like mad to pull back the professional persona she'd been so keen to promote.

'How very diligent of you. Well, to be honest, I'm not in the mood for spilling my deepest, darkest secrets right now.' He took a step closer to her and dipped his head, his gaze capturing hers as something dangerous flashed in his eyes. 'I'd like to get to know you a bit more *intimately* first.'

'I'm not going to sleep with you,' she blurted out before she could stop herself, her nerves riding roughshod over her common sense.

He laughed out loud, shaking his head in mirth.

Jess just stood there dumbly, flushing hot with embarrassment.

What an idiot she was. Of course he wasn't talking about sleeping with her. She very clearly wasn't his type if the media reports of his affairs were anything to go by. From what she'd seen in the press—and at his studio—he was more of a leggy-blonde type of guy.

And that suited her just fine. Absolutely fine. Couldn't be finer.

'Don't worry, I'm taking a break from seducing innocent young journalists, so your virtue is safe with me,' he joked, his mouth quirked in a playful smile. 'I *am* interested in your body, Jess, but only on an artistic level.'

Jess pulled her arms across her chest. 'You can't blame me for being wary when you make provocative-sounding statements like that. You do have a reputation for being a bit...'

'A bit what?'

She paused, searching for the right word. 'Wild.'

He gave her a bemused grin. 'I promise to be on my best behaviour,' he said, making a crossing motion over his heart. 'And if I slip up you have my permission to *lick* me into shape.'

Oh, my God, the images he'd just conjured in her mind.

She really needed to get out of here before she totally lost her cool.

'Come over for dinner tonight at eight,' he continued, going over to a rock where he'd left his towel and swiping it along his long, lean arms, 'and we can get better acquainted.'

He flashed her one last beguiling smile before turning and walking away up the path, the bright drops of lake water that still clung to his broad back shimmering in the sunlight.

An overwhelming urge to pack up and go home, where she didn't have to deal with these weird and disturbing feelings he provoked in her, besieged her. But she wasn't going to leave. She was determined to keep her job at the magazine, no matter what it took. She was going to brazen it out here and ignore the blatant innuendos he seemed so keen to tease her into a jittery mess with.

He was a player all right, but she wasn't about to let him play *her*.

In total contrast to the villa where Xander was staying, her hotel was the most run-down, sleazy-looking pit Jess had ever had the misfortune to set eyes on. She could have sworn she saw a rat run around the corner of the building as she parked her hire car in the tiny, litter-strewn parking lot. The thought of it made her shudder. She wasn't good with rodents. Or spiders. Or any type of insect if she was totally honest.

It looked as if they were doing building works on the place, too, judging by the mess of rubble and steel piled haphazardly against the peeling walls of the hotel, but there didn't seem to be anyone doing any actual work out there. Jess prayed she wasn't going to be woken up in the early hours by workmen banging the hell out of the wall next to her head.

A disgruntled receptionist with long, lank hair and a sweat-stained blouse checked her in and handed over her key, motioning her to walk through the rather run-down reception to a door on the ground floor, next to what appeared to be a kitchen.

The Ritz it was not.

Her room wasn't in a much better state than the reception, but at least it had a decent-sized bed and its own en-suite bathroom—even if she did have to turn sideways when in it to get the door closed.

Okay, well, it was all she needed. She was only going to put up with it for two nights. Surely it wouldn't take longer than that to get enough info to write a decent piece on Xander?

Kicking off her shoes, she flopped down onto the bed, ignoring the unnerving sway of the bed frame, and pulled her mobile out of her back pocket. Time to do some more research on the man himself.

She'd already had a cursory look through the search engines for his name, but not much of any use had come up, mostly gossip pieces about the women he'd dated and the parties he'd made a scene at. In fact he seemed to have been in a constant state of drunken debauchery for an entire year. There were a handful of articles about his last couple of exhibitions as she trawled lower, though, the last of which had been a bit of a critical flop, as Pam had mentioned.

She wondered how his colossal ego had dealt with that. Judging by the press reports on him between now and then, not very well. He'd become belligerent and withdrawn with the press and, instead of producing more work to shut his critics up, he'd thrown himself into partying and womanising instead. In fact he didn't seem to have produced a single thing since that exhibition.

Interesting.

It was a soothing distraction focusing on work after the nerve-jangling meeting with Xander and her eyelids grew heavy as she relaxed into the soft mattress. Perhaps she could get forty winks in now to power herself up before having dinner with Xander tonight? She wanted to be at her sharpest when she faced him again. She had a sneaking suspicion he was deliberately trying to unsettle her so he could avoid having to answer any of her probing questions.

If he thought it was going to be that easy to get around her he had another think coming.

A loud scuttling sound—which seemed to be emanating from under the bed—made her sit bolt upright in alarm.

What the hell was that?

Out of the corner of her eye she thought she saw something dart from under the bed and disappear behind the vanity unit on the other side of the room.

Goosebumps pricked her skin as all the hairs on her body stood up as one in disgust. Ugh! Bugs! Quite possibly cockroaches.

Her spirits sank to the floor. How was she supposed

to sleep with large indeterminate creatures running around under her bed?

Taking care not to step on any of the little blighters, she dashed out of the room and back over to the reception and tried to persuade the woman to move her into a different room.

Denied.

It appeared—incredibly—that the hotel was fully booked.

Jess sighed and went back to her room, feeling frustrated and discombobulated. She couldn't afford to move out of this hovel—her savings wouldn't stand it—and she wasn't about to leave, not when the fate of her career was in the balance.

She was just going to have to grit her teeth and suck it up.

CHAPTER THREE

WHEN DINNER TIME rolled around, Jess drove back over to Xander's villa in an even more agitated state than when she'd left it, which didn't bode well for a relaxed and fruitful interview with him.

She hadn't anticipated having to conduct her interview over dinner either. She used to hate eating in front of other people after struggling with an eating disorder for most of her teens. Thankfully things had got a lot better on that front after she'd taken herself off for counselling during her time at university. After talking things through she'd been able to work out a way to deal with the feelings of shame and self-loathing that tipped her into comfort eating when she felt stressed and she hadn't had a relapse since.

She had a suspicion that eating in front of Xander was going to be a real test of her fortitude, though. He was just so *in your face* with his off-the-scale charisma and haunting good looks.

Damn him.

Rosa opened the door to her with a smile and showed her through to the huge living room, which was furnished with only a sofa, small drinks table and fireplace. There was an amazing coloured-glass chandelier hanging from the ceiling, which looked a bit like an exploding bouquet of long-stemmed flowers. Refracted shards of light from it bounced off the walls, giving the room the feel of a disco paused in time. Jess had never experienced anything like it. 'Xander's running a little late, but he'll be with you soon,' Rosa said, giving Jess a kind smile. 'Can I get you a drink?'

'Just some water, please,' Jess said, determined to remain sharp and focused that evening, which meant no alcohol for her. She didn't tend to drink much anyway—hating the way alcohol messed with her head—and she had a horrible feeling that just a sniff of the stuff tonight would be a disaster in terms of keeping her cool and collected front in place.

Rosa nodded and gestured to the sofa before leaving her alone in the room.

Jess chose not to sit down, nerves making her too edgy to stay still, and instead wandered around the room. She took a closer look at the beautiful marble fireplace and the amazing glass chandelier, shifting uncomfortably in her six-inch heels as she waited for Xander to materialise. She'd chosen these shoes at the last second thinking the extra height would give her a bit more confidence, but they were already killing her feet, which set her teeth on edge.

She was dragged out of her funk by the sight of Xander finally sauntering into the room, wearing a light blue linen shirt, open at the neck, dark combat trousers and a spellbinding smile on his face.

He really was the perfect specimen of a man.

Even the loose cut of his clothes couldn't conceal the fact he had a killer body underneath. No doubt those lean muscles were flexing and bunching under his shirt as he moved towards her. It made her mouth water to think of it.

How would he feel if she pressed her hands against his chest?

Hard and soft at the same time.

The tips of her fingers tingled in empathy with her thoughts and there was a disturbing rush of warmth in the depths of her pelvis. She had to practically cross her legs to dull the sensation in order to concentrate.

Not good, Jess. Not good.

How the heck was she going to get through the evening? Already the butterflies that had taken up residence in her stomach were flapping about like wild things, which meant her appetite was at approximately zero on the famished to sated scale.

'Welcome to my humble abode,' Xander said, giving her a generous smile as he came to a halt in front of her.

He seemed relaxed, insouciant even, as if he was anticipating a pleasant, gentle evening of good food and lively conversation.

Her blood fired round her veins at the realisation that this dinner might not be *quite* as awkward as she'd anticipated. She just needed to keep focused and keep him on her side in order to get him to open up and talk about things that would make her article sparkle.

'Take a seat,' Xander said, motioning to the huge red velvet-covered sofa in the middle of the room.

'Okay, thank you.' Jess sank down gratefully onto the soft cushions, glad to finally take the weight off her feet, and kept on sinking. The innards of the sofa were so soft she found herself nearly doubled in two with her knees up near her chin.

Not exactly ladylike.

'I'm really pleased you decided to come,' Xander said, flopping down next to her and almost catapulting her onto his lap. 'I think we can both get something useful out of our time together.'

He gave her such a loaded smile she could do nothing but stare back at him.

'Yes, I'm sure we can,' she finally managed to mumble through lips that seemed to be malfunctioning under the force of his charisma.

He slowly dropped his gaze to her mouth and the intensity of the atmosphere stepped up another notch.

Focus, Jess, focus.

She took in a deep breath. 'This is a wonderful room,' she said, trying like mad not to go to pieces as the fresh and delicious citrusy scent of his aftershave hit her nostrils. My, he smelt good. Perhaps she *was* hungry, after all? Only not for food.

Give it a rest, Jess. You're here to do a job, keep it professional. And he's the personification of danger, remember, which is not something you need in your life right now.

Wriggling along the sofa away from him and swivelling her knees into the gap she'd left, she attempted to put a defensive barrier between them, only to watch him reposition himself, mirroring her action so that their knees were almost touching. Her breath caught in her throat at what appeared to be a deliberate move to unsettle her and she had to look away to gather her courage.

She was *so* out of her comfort zone here.

Rosa arrived with a couple of flutes of strawberry Bellini, Jess's requested glass of water and a bowl of the most enormous olives Jess had ever seen, which she placed in front of them with a flourish.

'Dinner will be served in ten minutes,' she said, giving them both a gracious nod.

'Thanks, Rosa,' Xander replied, the deep smooth tone of his voice twisting through Jess's head like music. No wonder women seemed to throw themselves at him wherever he went—all he had to do was speak and she was a gibbering wreck. Imagine the effect if he decided to talk dirty to her.

A deep, low throb began to pulse in the depths of her pelvis at the thought and her face flamed with heat. Good grief, what was wrong with her self-control? It seemed to have totally abandoned her.

Jess hurriedly picked up a Bellini and took a sip, grateful for the distraction from dealing with Xander's overwhelming presence for a moment.

So much for her no-drinking rule.

But this was an emergency—she needed something to flatten out her nerves and lull her into a more relaxed state of mind if she was going to get through the evening with her sanity intact.

Turning back, she found he was studying her, a look of concentrated interest on his face. They stared at each other for a moment and Jess's heart hammered in the pause.

Had it suddenly got hotter? She could swear they'd turned the heat up and were directing it straight at her. She was damp with perspiration under her long-sleeved blouse and even the underside of her knees was sweating.

Umm, attractive.

Thank goodness this wasn't a real date because he'd have to *swim* to get close enough to kiss her at this rate.

'You have the most expressive face I've ever seen,' he murmured, a glint of mischief in his eyes. 'I'm going to have a lot of fun drawing you.'

Jess cleared her throat and sat up taller in her seat,

anxiety at the thought of having to model for him making her body hum with nerves.

'So how exactly do these things go? Do I just sit around for a couple of hours and you produce some amazing piece of art?'

He smiled. 'Not exactly. I prefer to hang out with my subjects for a bit until inspiration hits me. It can take a while to come up with the right idea and I like to play around with things for a while before committing paint to canvas. I'll do some sketches over the next few days and see what works.'

'The next *few days?* I wasn't expecting to be here for that long. I thought we could get this all wrapped up in a day. Two max. In fact I've booked a return flight for two days' time.'

He snorted. 'A day? If only I could work that fast. No, I usually need at least three or four days of planning. But don't worry, we can make it fun.' He gave her a slow wink that made her insides flip.

'What exactly do you mean by that?' The question came out sounding curter than she'd intended, so she chased it with an awkward smile.

He snorted, the corner of his mouth twisting up in mirth. 'Why are you so nervous, Jess?'

'I'm not nervous,' she said, the squeak in her voice totally giving her away.

He laughed, the sound rumbling low in his chest. 'Is my reputation really that bad?' He leant forward in a conspiratorial manner. 'Don't worry, I'm not going to rip your clothes off and ravish you—unless you ask me really nicely,' he added with a flirtatious eyebrow raised.

Was he *teasing* her now? He was. He *so* was. And she had absolutely *no* idea how to handle it.

This was exactly why she usually avoided men like him. They rattled her so badly she could barely function.

Mercifully, Rosa returned to call them for dinner then so she didn't have to scrabble around for an eloquent response to that little zinger.

'After you.' Xander gestured towards the other end of the hall.

'Great,' Jess said, already on her feet and making a move towards the doorway he'd motioned at, desperately trying not to skid in her shoes on the smooth marble floor. She could *feel* him behind her, as if he were giving off a pulse of sexual electricity that made the hairs on the back of her neck stand to attention.

Just as they reached the dining-room door her heel caught in a small hole in the marble and she stumbled forward, her arms flailing out at her sides as she tried to regain her balance.

Xander stopped her from falling flat on her face by darting forward and grabbing her arm and pulling her against his body for support.

Taking a hurried step away from the hard wall of his chest, she smoothed down her hair, then her skirt from where it had ridden up her legs, before flashing him a grateful smile. He watched her with an amused eyebrow raised. 'You okay?'

'Fine. Thank you.' She gave him a friendly but controlled nod. 'I'm not normally that clumsy, honestly.'

Xander laughed. 'Don't worry on my account. It's not often I get to play the knight in shining armour. It's usually *me* falling down drunk.'

'I'm not drunk, I only had a couple of sips…' she began to argue, horrified he'd think she was that much of a lightweight.

He held up a hand. 'I'm joking, Jess. Jeez, I've never met anyone so bad at taking a joke.'

'I c-can take a joke with the best of them,' she stuttered, picking a rogue hair off the sleeve of her blouse before turning to stare him defiantly in the eye.

Xander shook his head and grinned back at her. 'Do you think you can make it to the table without taking another tumble? I can give you a piggyback if you like.'

'I'll be fine, thank you,' she said. 'Wouldn't want to be responsible for putting your back out.'

He laughed. 'Never gonna happen. I'm as strong as an ox. See?' He braced his arms in front of him, mimicking the stance of a bodybuilder.

Jess couldn't help but laugh at him.

'Yeah, okay, He-Man, but I'll walk, thanks.'

He smiled back, and waved a hand, encouraging her to step to it. 'After you.'

The dining room was just as impressive as the living room with an enormous, highly polished dining table sitting pretty in the middle of the room, surrounded by what looked like twenty high-backed chairs.

Another enormous chandelier, this time made from hundreds of pieces of blown glass in the shape of a flock of birds, let out a warm, low light over the room.

'Wow, the light fixtures here are amazing,' Jess said, staring at it in wonder.

'Pretty cool, huh?' Xander said, stopping next to her to admire it, too. 'Roberto, who owns this place, made it. He's sickeningly talented.'

He was standing so close to her she caught another waft of his amazing citrusy scent, which sent an energised prickle right up her spine.

'How lovely of him to let you use his place,' she said, taking a careful step into the room, away from him.

'Yeah, he's a really generous guy. We worked on a couple of projects together a few years back, before we both started getting successful. He lets friends come and stay here when they need to escape for a bit.'

'So you're *escaping* right now?' she asked, turning back to look at him.

His expression closed over. 'I need a bit of space to concentrate on a new exhibition, away from the din of the city.'

'And away from the temptation of all those parties?' she said, raising a playful eyebrow, hoping he'd bite and give her a bit of gossipy goodness that she could incorporate into her article.

'Oh, I don't know. I'm sure I can find a party round here if I really want to,' he said, moving his shoulder in a circular motion as if trying to relieve a trapped nerve.

'Have you hurt your shoulder?' she asked.

'Nah, I'm just a bit tense from being bent over drawing today. Why, are you offering to rub it for me?' He flipped her a provocative grin.

'You don't want me giving you a massage—I'm terrible at it,' she said, smoothing a lock of hair behind her ear, then flipping it back out again so it swung back to join the rest of her bob. She had a horrible urge to hide her face from him. He was so confusing with his ability to flip the conversation from something innocuous into something that made her jitter with barely contained anxiety.

He gave her a questioning frown. 'I don't believe it. How can you be terrible at massaging?'

She shrugged. 'It's just not something I count as one of my talents.'

'Hmm.' He was looking at her with such an intense, searching stare it made her insides twist.

She wasn't used to dealing with such overt flirta-
tiousness. The men she'd dated in the past had been attractive guys, but nothing like the unwieldy package of
sexual energy that Xander Heaton embodied. He was
something else entirely.

Walking past her, he pulled out a chair from the table
and gestured for her to sit down.

She nodded her thanks and perched herself on the
edge of the leather-upholstered chair, folding her hands
on the tabletop and kicking off her shoes so she could
flex her aching feet under the table. She watched as he
pulled out the seat opposite and dropped into it with
a sigh.

'I'm curious. Why don't you give interviews any
more?' she said, hoping that if she just kept firing random questions at him he'd eventually give her some
straight answers.

He leant back in his chair and smoothed the front of
his shirt down with long, tanned fingers.

Jess watched the movement, fascinated by the simple
beauty of his hands, noting how his fingernails were
dark-rimmed with ingrained paint. There was something lovely about how his hands reflected exactly who
he was.

A warm and tingly feeling wound through her
belly—and lower—as her thoughts slid towards what
sort of mischief he could get up to if he put those amazing hands of his on her body.

She really needed to stop thinking about him like
this; it wasn't conducive to getting the best out of the
interview if all she could think about was how damn
sexy he was.

'I've had some bad experiences with the press twisting things I've said. They take things out of context

and make me sound like an idiot.' He leant forward in his chair. 'And I prefer to keep my private life just that—*private*,' he said, giving her a knowing smile and stretching out his legs under the table, his calf brushing gently against hers. 'But I'm sure I can trust you to give me a fair write-up, Jess, especially as I have the power to make you look bad, too. You don't want your *bad-hair day* hanging on someone's wall for ever, do you?'

Her breath seemed to be coming out in shorter gasps than normal, which was making her light-headed. Sucking in a deep, calming slug of air, she carefully moved her leg away from his and attempted to centre herself before responding.

'You wouldn't do that.' The shake in her voice made it clear she totally believed he *would*.

He laughed. 'Of course not. I'm only joking. I promise to be true to your character.'

She nodded slowly. 'So what happened last year to kill your muse?' she asked casually, glancing up at him through her lashes in the hope he'd answer without thinking.

He gave her such a *what the hell are you talking about?* look she shrank back into her seat in disgrace.

Okay, so it wasn't the most professional way to conduct the interview, but then again she had nothing to lose throwing out provocative questions. In fact, if she was going to get something juicy enough to satisfy Pamela she was going to have to push the boat right out and straight into enemy waters.

Xander must have thought he'd reacted a bit too strongly because he flicked her a smile and manipulated his body into a more relaxed posture.

'My muse isn't dead, just resting. I had a few years where I worked pretty intensively and I needed a break.'

'So taking a break had nothing to do with the reviews you had of your last exhibition, then?'

His expression darkened and he leant forward in his chair. 'You really think I care about the opinions of a few talentless hacks? I have zero respect for people who don't have the ability to produce their own art so spend their time and energy trashing other people's work instead. They're a waste of space and not something I'm willing to talk about again, so you can cross that one off your list of *probing questions for Xander.*' The cold resentment in his voice made her shiver.

Okay, lesson learned, she wasn't going to be able to rush this. Probably best to keep the conversation bland for now and build up to the more probing questions. After all, if he wanted more time to sketch her she could afford to take things slowly and build his trust in her before slipping him the leading questions.

Xander relaxed back into his chair and attempted to shake off the unsettling avalanche of anxiety that Jess's questions had buried him in. He really needed to keep his temper under control or she'd think she was onto a juicy story about how he felt about the press's less-than-favourable reaction to his last show.

He'd relived the hurt and anger of last year's glitch in his career over and over until it had nearly driven him crazy, and he was determined to get over this debilitating fear of failing again. He really didn't need her poking at that old wound when he was finally feeling the creative buzz again.

Jess leant back in her chair and studied him for a moment and he tensed, waiting to see whether he'd been successful at closing that line of questioning down.

'What does it feel like to be voted the fourth sexiest man in England?' she said finally, a mischievous eyebrow raised.

He smiled, relieved that she'd taken the hint and changed the subject.

'Actually I hear I'm third in the UK right now and it's a real honour.'

'I bet.' She shot him a judicious look. 'Any plans to up your rating? How much sexier do you think you'd need to be to reach number one, for example?'

He laughed. 'Quite a bit.'

She snorted and picked up her water, taking a quick sip. 'If you *did* get any sexier I think most women— and probably some men—would melt under the force of your charisma.'

He gave her a lazy grin, something warm and happy growing larger deep in his belly. 'You think I'm sexy?'

Her gaze shot away from him and she put her glass down hurriedly, managing to catch it awkwardly on her side plate and spilling water onto the tablecloth. 'I can see why other people think you are.' She didn't look back at him, but busied herself mopping up the spill with her napkin.

'But you don't *personally*?'

She still wouldn't look at him. 'I have odd tastes.'

'Odd?'

'Yeah, boy-next-door types, I guess. Men I feel comfortable to be with. Men who aren't going to outshine me wherever we go.'

'I can't image anyone outshining you.'

She raised a discerning eyebrow. 'You're sweet to say that, but I'm warning you now, I can smell B.S. a mile away.'

God, she was saucy when she got all strict.

'You're really something, you know that?' Xander

said, leaning forward and putting his elbows onto the table.

There was something about the wariness on her face that made him long to get behind that tight-lipped front she put up to protect herself. He was pretty sure there was a lot going on beneath the surface with Jess and he longed to find out what was driving it. He'd not met anyone as guarded—and seemingly immune to his charms—as her in a very long time.

He liked that about her. He liked it a lot.

And he was determined to shake the real her out from under those layers of protection.

'Okay, if you don't want to talk about your last exhibition let's try some quick-fire questions,' Jess said, ignoring his attempt at flirting her into submission and hoping her *slowly, slowly* approach would yield better results. If she could keep things light and seemingly unobtrusive he might just give her something without feeling as though he was.

Although, judging by the bemused look on his face, she suspected she was going to have a tough time getting him to take *any* of this seriously.

Shoving back his chair and balancing a foot on his knee, he waved at her to begin. 'Shoot.'

She cleared her throat and sat up straighter, pen poised over her notepad in readiness. 'Okay. Beer or wine?'

He raised an amused eyebrow. 'Tequila body shots.'

Heat rushed up her neck as a vision of him licking salt out of her belly button slammed into her head. She pushed it away quickly, hoping her expression hadn't given her away. She didn't want him to know how much he was getting to her.

'Favourite animal?' she ploughed on, not looking up from her pad.

'Tiger.' He growled and she glanced up to see him making clawing gestures with his hands.

She fought to keep her smile under wraps. 'Favourite way to travel?'

'Asleep.'

She sighed. Yup, he wasn't going to make this easy on her.

'What?' he asked, holding his hands up in mock offence. 'I hate travelling—it's tedious. I try to sleep through all my journeys.' He leant forward in his chair. 'I'm guessing you're one of those people who don't believe in power naps.'

'I can't sleep during the day.'

'What, never? You should practise. It's a useful skill.'

'I'm usually too busy *working* in the day.'

He grinned. 'Yeah, well, if you sleep as badly as me you need to master afternoon napping.'

'Have you always slept badly?' she asked, intrigued by the small snippet of personal information he'd let slip.

He shifted in his chair, switching his legs over and propping the other foot on the opposite knee, obviously annoyed at himself for slipping up and offering her a lead into something else he didn't want to discuss.

'I've always had strange sleep patterns.' He didn't look at her and she wondered why. Judging by the sudden tension in his body she'd swear he was lying.

'What is it that keeps you up in the night?' she pushed, determined to pursue this until he gave her something interesting she could use in the piece.

He glanced back at her, his expression now teasing.

'Usually the hot woman lying next to me.' He shot her another grin, but the smile didn't quite reach his eyes.

'Right. So what? All the partying you've become so famous for is to help you sleep? Wouldn't it be easier to take a sleeping pill?'

'I party hard to have fun. You've heard of that, right? Fun.' He gave her a slow, lazy smile as if he knew exactly what she did for fun. She thought about all the quiet nights in and cringed a little.

'Sadly, I don't have the opportunities or resources that you do,' she said, trying to keep the giveaway clip of indignity out of her voice.

Instead of responding, he got up and left the room, leaving her staring after him.

What the hell? Was this how he was going to act whenever she started on a line of questioning he wasn't comfortable with?

Before she had chance to get up and follow him out, he reappeared, sketch pad and pencil in hand.

Her stomach did a slow dive. 'What are you going to do with those?' she asked dumbly, suddenly hot with worry. He wasn't going to start sketching her *now*, was he?

'I needed a little predinner snack and these looked delicious,' he said, his voice laden with sarcasm.

Jess bristled. 'Do you really need to start doing that right now, here at the dinner table?'

'Why not? You brought your work to the table. Why can't I bring mine?'

She had no answer for that. He had a point.

Flattening her hair down with hands that no longer felt as if they belonged to her, she shuffled up straighter in her seat.

'Look, Xander, I'm not really comfortable...'

'Don't worry, you don't need to do anything differently, I just had an image I wanted to get down before I forgot it. I have to grab these little flashes of inspiration when they strike. Unfortunately, my muse isn't something I have any control over.'

'A bit like your libido,' she muttered, staring down at the table, unwilling to meet his eyes in case he saw how awkward he was making her feel.

He didn't make any reply to her jibe, but when she flicked her eyes up to check what he was doing she noticed a small curl to his lips, as if he was trying to suppress a smile. His gaze was fully focused on what he was doing, but as she watched him move the pencil fluidly over the paper he glanced up for a second and caught her staring.

She looked away quickly, heat burning her cheeks.

Rosa appeared in the doorway with plates of food and Jess breathed a sigh of relief when Xander put down his pad and ceased the impromptu sketching session.

Taking a deep breath, she tentatively started in on the scrumptious-looking salmon, asparagus and salad that Rosa placed in front of her. Her appetite seemed to have totally abandoned her now, but she wasn't going to let her insecurities get the better of her—no way. Even so, she hardly tasted a bite of the meal as she worked her way through it. It was as if her taste buds had packed up and gone on holiday, making everything she ate turn to dust in her mouth.

She put her cutlery down after managing only half of it, defeated.

'How was your food?' Xander asked, startling her as he laid his own knife and fork onto his empty plate.

'It was delicious. I really enjoyed it. There's just a bit too much for me here,' she said, feeling the heat of her discomfort flaring in her cheeks. Looking down, she re-alised her hands were trembling so she hid them under-neath the napkin on her lap, hoping he wouldn't notice.

'You know, I don't think I've ever met a journalist who was such an awful liar before,' Xander said, lean-ing back in his chair and putting his hands behind his head as he studied her. 'You looked like you were being tortured all the way through eating that.'

That did it.

The stress of attempting to stay calm around him, the pressure of potentially losing her job if she couldn't get him to play ball and his utter disrespect for her profes-sion all collided in her head, shooting her blood pres-sure to maximum.

'You know what, I didn't want to believe all the gos-sipy reports about you being an *arrogant idiot*, but I can see now they're totally on the money.'

He stared back at her, eyebrows raised and a mus-cle twitching in his jaw, but didn't say a word in his defence.

Had she blown it losing her cool like that? Was that the end of this little fiasco? She felt as if the whole thing had spun out of her control and she had no idea how to claw it back.

But instead of telling her to get out of his house, he picked up his sketchbook and pencil again and started to scribble away as if she weren't even in the room.

She sat for a minute or two, waiting to see whether he'd speak to her again, but he steadfastly ignored her.

'Look, I'm sorry for losing my temper. I'm just feel-ing a bit…out of my depth at the moment.'

Still nothing. Not even an acknowledgement that she'd spoken.

'O-okay, then…well…' she stuttered, scrunching up

the napkin from her lap and dropping it onto the plate in front of her. 'On that bombshell, I'll let you get on with your picture and get back to my hotel.'

Perhaps once she'd had a good night's sleep everything would look rosier in the morning and they could start afresh. She tried not to shudder as she remembered the insect-infested room that awaited her.

He said nothing as she slid out of her seat, stooping to pick up her shoes. She decided against putting them back on, mainly because it would delay her leaving, but also because her poor aching feet would have screamed at her to stop torturing them if she had.

'Goodnight, Xander,' she said to the top of his head before walking away from him, not daring to look back and catch the look of amusement that *had* to be taking over that unnervingly handsome face of his.

Slumping back against his chair and dropping his sketch pad and pencil onto the table, Xander watched Jess stalk out of the dining room in her stockinged feet, her shoes swinging from her fingers at her side.

A slow burn of shame worked its way through him.

Perhaps he'd pushed things a little too far with that last comment? Judging by her violent reaction to it, *she* certainly seemed to think so. He'd found it amusing to play with her when he'd realised she was actually more nervous around him than she'd previously let on, but he really should apologise tomorrow and see if he could get her back on side once she'd calmed down.

He wouldn't usually entertain the idea of letting a journalist get anywhere close to him, but he liked Jess. There was something about her that fascinated him, something about her stoic determination not to let him get to her that made him want her more than anyone he'd met in a very long time. The thought of drawing her out of that brittle shell she protected herself with was thrilling. It did something disconcerting to him, causing a twisting heat to take him over and make him reckless—something he'd been determined not to be again until his new exhibition was in the bag, but teasing her had been such a turn-on. He'd love to see how she responded to a serious onslaught of flirting and whether he could change her mind about not wanting to sleep with him. He'd been surprised and not a little rankled when she'd said that earlier, and the narcissist in him wanted to prove her wrong. It had been a long time since a woman had turned him down, which made it a point of pride.

He knew she felt *some* sort of attraction to him because of the unconscious way she responded when she was around him. Her pupils flared when she looked his way and her body language became charmingly jerky and more drawn towards him.

So why was she fighting it so hard?

He had no idea, but he was going to enjoy finding out.

Jess got back to her hotel room in a state of nervy agitation.

Her dinner with Xander had shot her adrenaline levels into the red, but now she'd calmed down she felt utterly exhausted by it all.

Lying in her bed, she allowed her thoughts to skip over what had happened earlier. A small voice in her head started to whisper something about overreacting a bit. Hot embarrassment trickled through her as she thought about how uncomfortable she'd felt around Xander and how that had *perhaps* made her act a *little* more edgily than normal. He hadn't actually said or done anything *that* bad. He was clearly deliberately trying to wind her up—and she'd let him succeed.

Rubbing a hand across her scalp, she tried to wake up her sluggish brain. What the heck was she doing? She needed to *chill* and stop going at Xander like a harpy with a headache if she had any chance of getting him to trust her enough to talk about anything personal.

She was a smart, educated woman with good conversation skills; she could get what she needed for the article if she just stopped jumping down his throat every time he opened his mouth. No way was she going back to Pamela without something sensational to use in the magazine.

She was going to have to work harder at it, be tenacious.

It was totally doable.

As long as she could keep this crazy compulsion to get up close and personal with him out of her head.

Another scuttling sound, this time from the corner of the room, made her sit up and flick the bedside light back on. She couldn't see anything, but somehow that was worse. What if the insects crawled up the sides of the bed and found their way under the covers with her? The thought of it made her heart hammer and her skin crawl with disgust. Wrapping the sheets round her like a cocoon, she tried not to think about it and relax into sleep.

The scratching noise came again, this time from the other side of the room. Finding her earphones from her handbag, she stuffed them into her ears, connected them to her MP3 player and turned the music right up. Putting the pillow over her head, she hoped, would be enough to ward off any uninvited bedfellows.

Her thoughts drifted back to Xander and what he

would be doing right now. Perhaps he'd be in the shower, washing off the grime of the day, water and suds cascading down that impressive body of his as he soaped himself down?

The mere thought of it made her blood fire round her body again.

Her legs were twitching now as she lay there desperately trying to turn her thoughts to something innocuous so she could drift into a much-needed sleep.

Between the apprehension of dealing with Xander again and the worry about warding off the bugs, she seemed to have kicked herself back into a state of anxious alertness.

Sighing, she burrowed deeper into the covers and started counting sheep. She had a horrible feeling it was going to be a long night.

CHAPTER FOUR

XANDER HAD TO check the address of the hotel that Rosa had given him twice before he finally concluded he was in the right place. Was Jess really staying in this dump?

An unfriendly receptionist finally gave him Jess's room number and he walked along the grimy corridor and banged on her door with an unnerving sense of discomfort.

He'd woken up early that morning after a dream about Jess where she'd been buried under an avalanche of snow and he'd not been able to get close enough to rescue her. It was the most bizarre thing he'd ever dreamt—not least because he barely knew her—and the sense of loss it provoked had left a dragging sorrow in his chest that unnerved him so much he'd had to get straight up and go for a walk to clear his head.

Apparently his subconscious was feeling very guilty about how he'd treated her the night before. So, here he was, cap in hand and ready to apologise for his insensitivity in the hope he hadn't driven her away for good.

The door finally swung open to reveal a rather dishevelled-looking Jess, still in her pyjamas and with her normally immaculate bob of hair sticking up wildly around her pale face. The dark bags under her eyes made him suspect she hadn't slept well either.

Her face went from ghostly pale to beet-red in the space of a second when she realised it was him at the door and her hands flew straight up to flatten down her thatch of hair.

'Xander? What are you doing here?'

'I came to invite you over for breakfast and to say sorry for being an idiot last night.'

Jess stared at him in wide-eyed astonishment. 'Wow. Am I dreaming or did Xander Heaton just *apologise* to me?'

He snorted and leant against the doorjamb, watching in amusement as she took a stumbling step back into the room.

'It's real. Consider me humbled.'

She dipped her head and gave him a genuine smile. 'Apology accepted. Thank you for coming all the way over here. That's very decent of you.'

He batted her praise away, but acknowledged the feeling of satisfaction it brought, relieved she seemed to have forgiven him for his egotism. 'You were right. I was being an idiot.'

'Yeah, well, I wasn't exactly sweetness and light last night either,' she said, pulling her arms tightly across her chest, which only drew his attention to the large swell of her breasts. 'I'm sorry for being so narky.'

'Okay. So we're both sorry. That's great. Let's put it behind us.'

'Good idea.'

They stood looking at each other and an awkward silence crept up, making the air between them hum with tension.

'Nice place you have here,' Xander said, in an attempt to break it, shooting her a mischievous grin.

Her shoulders tensed. 'Yeah, it was the only room I could find at short notice.'

There was a loud scratching noise that seemed to be coming from inside the wall next to him.

He frowned hard. 'What the hell is that?'

She shrugged, her expression giving away her own disgust. 'Cockroaches, I think.'

The thought of her staying here in such awful conditions made him shudder. No wonder she looked as though she hadn't slept all night. A sudden overwhelming urge to protect her hit him like a hammer to the chest.

'You can't stay here. There must be somewhere else available?'

'There isn't. I looked. Everywhere else is fully booked or totally out of my price range.'

'Isn't the magazine stumping up for your accommodation?' he asked.

She shifted uncomfortably from foot to foot. 'There isn't the budget to put me up somewhere expensive. I'm just a junior staffer,' she said sheepishly, clearly worried he'd be offended that they hadn't sent their top reporter to interview him.

The flash of vulnerability did something to his insides, making him squirm in sympathy for her.

'Pack up your stuff. You're staying with me.'

She blinked at him in surprise. 'What?'

'I have four spare bedrooms at the villa. It's ridiculous for you to stay in this dump when there's so much room at my place.' He held up his hands, palms forward, when she frowned and started to shake her head.

'Rosa's there most of the time and the bedrooms have locks on the doors so you don't need to worry about me taking advantage of you.' He flipped her a grin in the hope she'd believe him. He couldn't in all conscience let her stay here any longer. The place was disgusting and he hated the thought of her having to put up with it for a moment longer when it was no skin off his nose for her to stay with him.

'But don't you want your privacy?' she hedged, rocking back on her heels.

He flapped a casual hand at her. 'There's enough room at the villa for us not to feel like we're in each other's pockets. You're going to be spending most of your time there anyway, right?'

She took a moment to think it over, staring down hard at the floor.

'I'll wait for you in Reception,' he said, moving back towards the door. 'Rosa's making breakfast so we'd better get back there soon.' He hoped his authoritative tone would tip her into action. He suspected she needed quite a bit of pushing to get past her stubbornness.

After five minutes of pacing up and down in the reception area, he finally saw her appear out of her room, now fully dressed, and walk down the corridor towards him wheeling a small suitcase, her shoulders drawn forward and her head dipped with tiredness.

The dull grey, shapeless linen trouser suit she'd put on today did nothing to express the feistiness he'd seen the previous night—it swamped her frame, diminishing her impact with its banality. Why on earth did she choose to dress like that when she had such passion inside her?

He wondered idly what her body looked like underneath those baggy layers. Soft and inviting and too tantalising not to touch, he imagined. He'd love the opportunity to find out for sure.

'Okay. I'd like to take you up on your kind offer,' she

said, coming to a halt in front of him, her chin tipped up defiantly as if she was afraid he'd think less of her for appearing so vulnerable. On the contrary, the fact she was daring enough to accept his help only made him like her more.

'Great, give me your bag and I'll meet you outside,' he said, taking the suitcase from her. She didn't stop him, clearly too tired today to put up a fight.

He waited outside by the car while she checked out, feeling the warmth of the early-morning sun seeping into his skin. Just being away from the city was already having a positive effect on him. The pace of life here was calming and he could feel the tension beginning to drain away. All he needed to do now was to utilise the growing sense of calm and the little flashes of inspiration Jess seemed to incite in him whenever she was around, and he could start to rebuild the confidence in his work he'd been missing.

He couldn't even begin to explain to himself why she had such a big effect on him, but, hell, it didn't matter, as long as the inspiration stayed around long enough for him to begin to create something he was proud of again. Already the sketches he'd done of Jess and the ideas she'd inspired in him were head and shoulders above anything he'd produced in the last year. There was finally life to his drawing again. Instead of the unimaginative marks on paper he'd had to drag out of himself up until this point.

Bizarre that she'd been the one to draw that out of him. She was nothing like the type of woman he usually hung around with, but there was something so beguiling about her.

Glancing back at the hotel, he saw Jess come out and blink in the sunlight as she looked around for him.

He gave her a wave and she walked stiffly over in those crazy high heels of hers and grabbed her case from him.

'Okay. I'll see you back at the villa,' she said, already wheeling her case off to her own car, tension clear in her gait.

'See you back there in ten,' he said, ducking into the driving seat, impatient to get back for some well-earned breakfast and the opportunity to get to know this intriguing woman a little better.

When he arrived back at the villa, Rosa had already laid out the breakfast things on the terrace. Xander flopped into a seat and stared out at the spectacular view over the lake while he waited for Jess to arrive and join him.

She was only a couple of minutes behind him and he watched as she made her way gingerly over the path that ran around the house and came to a stop at the chair opposite where he sat.

'Thank you for rescuing me from that place. You're my hero,' she said, flashing him a subdued grin and flopping down into the chair with a sigh.

Was she serious? Or was this her personal brand of sarcasm?

Man, it was unnerving not being able to read her easily. Perhaps the crux of their problem was they didn't get each other's sense of humour yet?

He chose to think she really meant what she said and smiled, relaxing back into his chair and hooking his arm over the backrest. 'Actually, it *was* pretty heroic of me. I'm *not* a morning person and I got up a whole hour early to come and fetch you for breakfast.' He chased this statement with a grin so she knew he was only joshing her.

Was that a flicker of appreciation he saw in her eyes? He was surprised by how much he hoped so.

Rosa came back and poured them each a cup of coffee, then put a plate loaded with toast and fruit in front of them. Jess frowned at it for a second before popping a piece of melon into her mouth and chewing it for rather longer than necessary before swallowing it.

'I'd like to sketch you this morning, when we've finished breakfast,' he said, before taking a long sip of the strong, aromatic coffee.

Her gaze shot to him, her eyes suddenly wild and uncertain.

'Really?' She cleared her throat, brushed some imaginary crumbs off her fingers, then smoothed her hands over her lap. 'Okay.'

He frowned at her reaction. 'What is it with you? You seem to be in a perpetual state of apprehension.'

She pushed her chair back and stood up so suddenly it made him jump. 'I'm fine. Really.' She gave him a shaky grin. 'I'm going to get settled in my room, have a shower and psych myself up before we start if you don't mind.'

He watched her walk away. Her body was rigid and her hands clenched at her sides as she moved awkwardly in her heels.

What the hell had he said wrong now?

After finding her outrageously luxurious room—which she investigated thoroughly before even taking her jacket and shoes off—Jess spent a while carefully unpacking her suitcase and hanging up her clothes in the enormous walk-in wardrobe. The soothing action of tidying was a welcome relief from dealing with the intensity of Xander's charismatic presence and she took her sweet time over it in order to stall having to go back outside again and sit for his picture.

Her small collection of clothes looked sad and limp and rather pathetic all by themselves on the enormous rail and she shut the door hurriedly on them, not entirely sure where the sudden dragging feeling of gloom had come from.

It must be down to not having slept all night.

When Xander had suggested she move in here with him, her first instinct had been to categorically dismiss the idea, but with her head feeling as if it were stuffed with cotton wool and her body aching with tiredness she'd actually been pathetically grateful when he'd insisted on it. Just the thought of spending another sleepless night in that awful hotel had made her insides clench and squirm.

She'd been surprised at his offer, considering how resistant he'd been to giving her anything personal of himself the previous night. Perhaps she'd looked so pathetic when he'd found her there he'd had a crisis of conscience?

Anyway, whatever his reasons, logically it would be a whole lot easier to stay in the same place as Xander as it meant she could get a really good feel for how he spent his days while he worked on his paintings.

She took a hot, reviving shower in the beautiful, mosaic-tiled en-suite bathroom and dressed in her most comfortable clothes: a pair of indigo boyfriend jeans and a loose, long-sleeved, white cotton T-shirt and slipped her feet into a pair of flip-flops.

Taking one last, deep breath, she went back out to the garden to find Xander, ready for the session.

Blood thundered through her veins at the thought of him scrutinising her from every angle, and flashbacks from being bullied about her weight when she was younger flittered through her mind, but she refused to feel cowed by those awful memories. It had been a long time since she'd let her eating disorder get its teeth into her, and she'd come so far since then. She refused to let it drag her under again.

Xander was sitting on the terrace with his sketch pad and pencils, making large swirling motions over the paper. He tilted his head and smiled, eyebrows raised, as she drew closer to him and she wrapped her arms around her middle and gave him her bravest smile back. She had no idea what he must be thinking right now and blood pounded in her head as her agitation increased.

Suck it up, Jess. You're doing this to save your career, remember?

If she could get through this modelling debacle, hopefully she'd have more opportunities to pump Xander for information.

The thought of 'pumping' in relation to Xander almost made her lose her cool for a second and she had to suck in a deep breath to steady herself. The low throb of arousal refused to budge from where it had nestled itself between the apex of her thighs, and she had to concentrate on putting one foot in front of the other to stop herself from swivelling on the spot and making a run for it.

She sat uncomfortably in the chair opposite him, with the lake behind her, the sun hot on her already heated skin. Her muscles were so twitchy she wouldn't be at all surprised to find she was visibly vibrating with tension.

Xander looked up and studied her for a moment, sketch pad on his knee, his bright eyes searching her face.

She wound her fingers together and placed them carefully on her lap, looking away over his shoulder in an attempt to distract herself from the discomfort of being studied so thoroughly by a man who made her insides jump and writhe as if they were filled with snakes.

'Relax, Jess. Anyone would think I was about to torture you.'

'I have no idea why you'd want to draw *me*,' she said, attempting to relax her shoulders into some sort of normal posture.

Xander laughed. 'You're much more attractive than you think you are, you know.'

She shot him a puzzled scowl. 'How the hell do you know how attractive—or not—I think I am?'

He didn't seem at all fazed by her snippy tone. 'I can see it in your body language. You don't believe in yourself.' He leant in closer. 'You know, you shouldn't worry so much about what everyone else thinks; just believe in how amazing you are.'

'That would be a lot easier if I *was* amazing.' She flipped him a grin, but he frowned, clearly unimpressed with her response.

'How can you not know how gorgeous you are?' he murmured.

The penetrating look he gave her made something awaken low in her pelvis.

Oooh.

'You need to let out the joy.' He didn't shift his gaze from her face, keeping her attention locked to him.

She laughed in lust-addled bewilderment. 'The joy?'

'You know. The place where a genuine smile comes from.'

She looked at him blankly. 'How do I find such a place?'

'Okay, think about the last time you felt happy and follow the feeling.'

She gave him a sceptical look.

'Humour me,' he said.

Sighing, she wiped her sweaty palms on the sides of her jeans. She didn't want him to see how nervous she was about being the centre of attention like this. Her pulse ticked loudly in her ears.

Sensing she was likely to lose this particular battle, and interested to see if the experiment worked, she sighed and shut her eyes, doing as he said, trying to capture the feeling of delight she'd experienced when Pamela had offered her the job on the magazine. She tried to pinpoint where the feeling emanated from, locating it somewhere deep in her chest where it pulsed low and hot.

'Okay,' Xander said. 'Now look right at me and let your eyes tell me how you're feeling.'

She took a second to centre herself, then did as he said, staring into his striking green-blue eyes and trying to communicate how she felt through the power of her expression.

'Not bad, but you need to stop worrying about what I'm thinking of you and let me *see* you.'

Heat crept up her neck. 'I have no idea how to do that.'

He was looking at her so intently she thought she might pass out. Getting up from his chair, he knelt in front of her. 'What are you hiding from?' he murmured, tucking a lock of hair behind her ear, leaving her skin supersensitised and tingling where he'd touched her.

She finally plucked up the courage to look at him and their gazes locked.

Heart pummelling her chest, Jess willed herself not

to look away this time. He was close to her, so close she could smell the fresh, citrusy smell of him, mingling with the heat of his body.

He was looking at her differently, she was sure of it. Not that she could put her finger on exactly what made her think that. It was a feeling. An unsettling, exciting, monstrous feeling she was afraid to acknowledge.

The feeling seemed to peak, swiftly followed by an overwhelming tiredness and she tried to—unsuccessfully—stifle a yawn.

Xander laughed quietly. 'Okay, I can see you're exhausted so I'm going to release you from the torture.' He sat back on his haunches.

Jess let out a loud sigh of relief. 'Thank God for that,' she murmured.

He frowned at her. 'You really don't enjoy being sketched, do you?'

She looked back at him, battling with the mixture of shame and defiance that coursed through her. 'I hate it.'

'Why?'

Sighing, she looked off towards the vast sparkling expanse of the lake, giving herself a moment to gather her wits. She wanted to tell him, so he'd know she wasn't just being freaky. 'My mum was a model in the seventies and she had this crazy idea that I would be one, too. Unfortunately, she ended up with a chubby, odd-looking child who hated being thrust into the limelight.' She laughed, hoping to sound flippant and unaffected, but instead managing to sound false and strained.

'It didn't stop her from dressing me up like a doll from the age of four and making me parade around in those awful beauty pageants you see on shockumentaries sometimes, though,' she ploughed on, unwilling to let Xander see how shaky she was about telling him this. 'I absolutely hated them, but she made me do it until I was old enough to categorically refuse. I always came last in those things and the constant look of disappointment on her face would make me physically ill.' She snorted, but still couldn't bring herself to look at Xander. 'Ever since then I've hated being looked at and judged. I prefer to blend into the background.' She shrugged, hoping she hadn't completely blown things with him. After his kindness that morning she felt as if she owed him an explanation about her reticence to be drawn. She didn't want him to think she was just being a prima donna about it.

When she finally plucked up the courage to meet his gaze her insides swooped at the expression of compassion on his face.

'So why did you agree to come here and go through with this if it meant putting yourself through so much torment?' he asked gently.

Xander held his breath, waiting to hear what would spill from those luscious lips of hers.

Say it's because you like me and want to spend more time getting to know me. The intensity of the need to hear those words shocked him.

Where had *that* thought come from?

She paused, staring back at him, a whole gamut of expressions running over her face.

'Because I need this interview with you so I can impress my editor.' She looked as though she was going to say more, but then clamped her mouth shut.

He snorted in frustration, the tension of the moment broken by her utter refusal to tell him what he wanted to hear.

His determination to win her over tripled.

Getting up, he braced himself against the arms of her chair, gathering his strength to leave without pulling her towards him and planting a reassuring kiss on those soft-looking lips first.

She was a total contradiction. On the one hand self-assured and feisty, but on the flip side withdrawn and uncertain.

'I'm going to go and work in the studio for a while and you should try and catch up on your sleep, but we should go out for dinner tonight. There's a great restaurant in Salò I want to try.' His rebellious gaze dropped back to her full, inviting mouth and he had to force himself to look away before he lost his cool and succumbed to the urge to drop his mouth onto hers, just to see how she'd react.

She gazed back at him, her eyes wide and utterly mesmerising.

'Okay, I'd like that.'

He tipped her a nod. 'Great. Let's go about eight o'clock.'

'Eight's great,' she said, nodding once.

'See you later.' He pushed himself up straight and strode away from her, forcing himself to keep his eyes front and centre and his unsettling hunger well and truly in check.

For now.

He could tell he was going to have to play the long game to get in with Jess, but the thought of it buoyed him.

He enjoyed a challenge.

After taking a long reviving nap, Jess spent the remainder of the day taking photos of the amazing villa and jotting down ideas for her article on Xander.

The reprieve he'd given her earlier had been a welcome relief, but she knew if she was going to get him to open up she was going to have to give more of herself than she'd originally anticipated. He'd responded really kindly to her confession about her hatred of being the centre of attention and she'd felt as if laying herself bare like that had actually endeared her to him.

She guessed that as an artist he needed to be able to see more than surface level, too.

But it was a dangerous game she was playing. She couldn't allow herself to get swept up in feeling as if there were more of a connection between them than there was. He was famous for his short, sharp affairs with his muses and she couldn't allow herself to get carried away and imagine there was any kind of romance to the situation.

Xander was a fantastic flirt but surely he didn't mean anything by it? He was just trying to get her to relax so she'd give him what he wanted.

He was clearly a very smart guy who played to his strengths.

After staring at her meagre collection of clothes for a few minutes, she shunned the grey linen suit—too formal—and her jeans—too informal—for the only other semisuitable thing for dinner out that she'd brought with her: a long, light wool jumper and black cotton trousers. It was a totally over-the-top outfit for a summer's evening but she hadn't anticipated needing anything for dining out. Her wardrobe at home didn't contain any decent 'going out' clothes any more anyway. Not since she'd moved to London and didn't have the money or energy to go out in the evenings.

Whatever. It would have to do. This wasn't a date, it was her job, so it shouldn't matter what she looked like.

Eight o'clock came and went and she found herself pacing the hall, her senses on high alert for any sign of Xander as she waited.

Finally, he appeared, his hair gleaming and pushed back away from his face as if he'd just stepped out of the shower. The casual, off-duty appearance did something funny to her insides. It made him more human somehow, more touchable.

As he got closer she noticed he smelt as if he'd just stepped out of the shower, too, all clean and fresh with a dark, musky undertone from some body product or other.

Even if he was the most delicious thing she'd ever encountered, she shouldn't lose sight of the fact he'd left her hanging around in the hall like a sad Muppet when he was the one who'd set the time to meet for dinner, then turned up late. She pursed her lips as he stopped in front of her, determined not to let his charisma beat her into submission. 'I was expecting you fifteen minutes ago.'

He grinned, knocking the ferocity right out of her. 'You look just like the headmistress of the school I was expelled from when you do that. Although that expression looks a lot sexier on you.'

Despite the smile tugging at her mouth, she somehow managed to raise a judicious eyebrow. 'I consider lateness to be rude, but then what else should I expect from such a *bad boy*?'

His mouth twitched at the corner but he held up both hands and dipped his head in acquiescence. 'It's a fair cop. You're right; it was rude of me to be late.'

She gave him a nod, trying to appear as if she were used to handling men like him every day.

'Let's go,' he said, opening the front door and gesturing for her to exit first.

They walked over to his car, which was parked under a small wooden awning covered in fragrant-smelling honeysuckle.

Jess was surprised and a little taken aback when Xander opened the passenger door for her and waited until she'd got in before closing it behind her. Was he on his best behaviour now she'd pointed out his rudeness? Could she really be having that much of an impact on him?

'What a gentleman,' she said after he'd walked round to the other side and slid into the driving seat.

'You don't mind that, then?' he asked. 'Some women hate having doors opened for them.'

'I don't mind at all. I consider it good manners. I'd do the same for you, though, if I got to the car first.'

He smiled and gave her a courteous tip of the head before slipping the car into gear and setting off.

'Did you book a table?' she asked.

He flipped her a grin. 'No, but they'll fit us in, don't worry about that.'

There was a queue five couples deep when they pulled up outside the vine-covered trattoria in Salò.

'Ah, bother it,' Jess said, her heart sinking. She really didn't fancy spending the next hour in such close proximity to Xander, driving round looking for somewhere else that could fit them in. Why hadn't he just booked a table?

Xander seemed blithely unconcerned as he parked the car in the trattoria's car park and opened his door to get out.

Jess followed him out into the warm evening air.

When he turned to look at her, she opened her mouth to ask him what they were going to do, but before she could utter a word he held up a hand to silence her.

'Give me a second to speak to the maître d',' he said, backing away from her towards the open door to the trattoria.

Striding confidently past the queue of future diners, he disappeared into the restaurant, leaving Jess gaping after him.

Everyone in the queue turned to look at her and she had to pull her phone out of her bag and pretend to be checking for messages so they wouldn't see how embarrassed she was.

Xander returned a minute later and beckoned her to follow him.

She hurried after him as he walked past the queue of people again, giving them all a friendly smile.

Every one of them smiled back at him. He was clearly allowed to push in front of them without causing any complaints.

Oh, to be that casually confident about things.

The maître d' met them at the door and ushered them inside to a small table at the back.

The trattoria was hot with the collected warmth of bodies and heat from the wood-fired stone pizza oven in the corner, and Jess's stomach rumbled as the amazing aromas of Italian food hit her nostrils.

'So they just happened to have this table free?' she asked after they'd seated themselves in heavy, highly decorated wrought-iron chairs and been handed menus by their waiter.

'No, but they made room for us.'

'I don't even know what that means,' Jess said, holding up her hands.

Xander grinned. 'Sometimes fame has its perks.'

Jess chose what she was going to eat quickly—a delicious-sounding chicken salad—and looked up to watch Xander as he studied the menu.

She had one of those disquieting moments where she seriously wondered whether she was dreaming this all up. If anyone had told her this time last week that she'd be in Italy, dining opposite Xander Heaton, she'd have told them to get their head checked. Even more baffling than the arbitrariness of her situation was the fact she felt as if she belonged here with him—that their camaraderie earlier had somehow taken their relationship up a level.

He glanced up and caught her staring at him.

'Everything okay, Jess?'

She flushed in embarrassment at being caught out. 'I'm fine. Just thinking how strange it is to be sitting here with you.'

'Strange?' He looked puzzled at her choice of word.

'Good strange. Not the sort of thing that ever happens to me. I live a pretty uneventful life usually.'

He leant back in his chair and considered her for a moment. 'Believe it or not, my life can be pretty dull, too. Especially when I spend a lot of time holed up on my own working on my paintings. That's why I like working with models. Having you around is a welcome relief from the usual boredom, to be honest.'

She raised her eyebrows and sat up, crossing her arms in front of her. She'd never considered his life could be like that, not when, according to the papers, he seemed to live such a hedonistic existence. 'That doesn't sound like a fun way to live.'

'It's not.'

'So why do you do it?'

* * *

Jess's question made Xander pause. It had been a long time since anyone had got close enough to ask him a question like that. He usually held journalists at arm's length when they were after personal details and none of the women he'd dated recently seemed interested in the *why*, only in what he could offer them in the *now*. But he found he wanted to talk to her about this side of him. Perhaps to prove to her he wasn't the cold-hearted playboy she clearly had him pegged as.

'It's my calling. What I feel I'm meant to be doing with my life. It makes life worth living. I think I'd wither and die if I had to go and work in an office every day.'

She smoothed a hand over her perfectly straight hair, which distracted him for a second as he wondered what it would feel like to run his own hands through it. It would be soft and silky as it slid through his fingers; he was sure of it.

'Are you worried about how your next exhibition's going to be received?' she asked, pulling him rudely out of his hair-fondling fantasy.

Get it together, Xander, for goodness' sake.

He shifted in his chair, going for relaxed nonchalance while he considered her question carefully, giving himself a few moments to formulate an evasive, but meaty answer. Apparently she was going to keep hammering at this line of interrogation and he was going to have to watch what he said in front of her.

'I'm walking on a knife-edge the whole time. There are hundreds of new faces appearing each year, desperate to step into the limelight. I have to produce something pretty damn special every time or I'll sink. That's a lot of pressure right there.'

'What do your parents think about your success?' she asked, looking down as she realigned the position of her cutlery on the table in front of her.

Clearing his throat, he put on the indifferent smile he'd perfected over the years. 'They're both dead.'

She looked up sharply. 'Oh, Xander, I'm so sorry. So you're on your own?'

'Yup. It's just me and my *massive ego* now.'

Her cheeks flushed an adorable shade of pink. 'Look, sorry about that. In my defence, I called it as I saw it at the time.'

He smiled. 'You called it right. I was being a tool.'

She pushed her knife too far back on the table and it fell onto the floor. After reaching down to rescue it, she swiped her hair away from her flushed face before giving him an embarrassed grimace and shuffling her chair closer to the table.

Their food arrived and they both tucked in, neither of them saying a word for a couple of minutes. His lasagne was delicious and it didn't take him long to make inroads into it.

Realising he was being rude concentrating on his food and not making conversation, he nodded at the half-eaten salad on her plate. 'Good?'

'Great,' she said, popping a piece of tomato into her mouth.

'So, Jess, tell me more about you. Are you married?' She must have swallowed her tomato the wrong way because she coughed and spluttered on it, her eyes watering as she fought to get her breath back.

Granted, it was more personal and direct than anything he'd previously asked and rather out of the blue, but he really wanted to know more about her.

'No,' she said finally, shaking her head and looking down at the table.

He was surprised by the relief he felt. 'Partner?'

'Not for a couple of years now.'

'Oh? Why did you split up—if you don't mind me asking?' He stood the ends of his cutlery on the table and gave her his full attention, intrigued as to how someone as attractive as Jess could have stayed single for so long.

She put her own cutlery onto her half-full plate before looking up at him. 'He was a nice enough guy, but he didn't make my heart sing.'

'You mean he didn't do it for you in the sack?'

Her attempt at a casual shrug was the worst bit of acting he'd ever seen.

'We didn't really click,' she muttered, not looking him in the eye. He wondered what she wasn't telling him. Had the guy abused her in some way? Just the thought of it made him suddenly inexplicably angry. Under that tough, shielded exterior, there was undoubtedly some deeply ingrained insecurity lurking. He'd seen flashes of it already and imagined he'd see more and more, the longer she stuck around.

'Anyway, my turn. How come you're not settled down with a partner?' she said, clearly wanting to change the subject and shift the attention back onto him.

'Serious relationships aren't my thing. I like variety. And I like sex. Lots and lots of sex,' he teased, wanting to get back to the light, flirtatious atmosphere they'd had earlier.

He wasn't sure what Jess was thinking now. Her huge, dark eyes seemed to have taken on a faraway look and her mouth was drawn back in a faintly twisted grimace as though her smile had gone wrong somewhere along the line.

He'd made her uncomfortable with his suggestive comment and seemingly not in the way he'd intended.

He really shouldn't be thinking about her like this, not when he'd promised himself he was taking a break from what the press liked to refer to as his philandering ways, but it was almost *impossible* when she looked the way she did, sitting there all buttoned up and tempting in front of him. He wanted to peel back her layers and peek at what was underneath. Hell, who was he kidding? He wanted to tear her clothes off right there in the restaurant and feast on her like a starving man.

She fiddled with the napkin on her lap, her eyes downcast again.

'I'm just going to find the bathroom,' she said suddenly, dumping the napkin on the table, pushing her chair back and going to stand up, then jerking to a stop, midrise, and sitting back down again, a look of shock on her face.

'Jess? What's wrong?'

'Um, I think my top's caught on the chair. I don't seem to be able to move.'

He couldn't help but laugh at her predicament, until he noticed the look of utter horror on her face. She tried standing up again, but the wrought-iron chair kept her in her place. Her eyes were wide with worry now.

'I'm stuck!'

He got up and scooted round to the back of her chair to find that some of the loops of her knitted top had somehow wound themselves around the swirls of the patterned metal back.

'Sit still, I'll get you free,' he said, trying to get his hands down between the narrow gap between her body and the back of the chair. He worked on the caught bits for a few moments, feeling the heat of Jess's humiliation burning into him as she sat as still as she could.

His large, clumsy fingers couldn't get the loops out from where they were caught in the iron maze, which seemed to have inexplicably closed around them.

'Jess, I'm sorry, it's no good, you're going to have to take your top off so I can get it free. I can't work in such a small space.'

He went to lift the hem of her jumper but she put her hand firmly on top of his, stilling the movement. He looked directly into her face and she shook her head hard, fear flashing in her eyes.

What the hell?

'I don't want you to see my body.' She was trembling.

He frowned. 'Why not?'

Twitching her head from side to side, she looked away from him.

'Jess? What's wrong?'

'Nothing, nothing…it's just…I can't take my top off in the middle of the restaurant.' Her voice came out all squeaky and panicked.

'Well, you're going to have to wear the chair home, then,' he said, exasperation at not being able to help her coming through clearly in his tone. 'Whatever possessed you to wear a wool top in this heat anyway?'

He stepped away as she started jerking madly away from the chair as if it would miraculously let her go if she showed enough determination.

'Jess, you're going to ruin…' But it was too late. There was a loud tearing noise as the delicate material came apart under the force of her tugging. Unfortunately some of the strands were still wound tightly around the chair back so the top still wouldn't come free.

Jess stilled, as if she'd been turned to stone, then pressed herself hard back against the chair to hide the ruined back of her top, staring up at him with such a look of abject misery it made his stomach turn over.

'Okay, this is ridiculous.' He pulled open the buttons on his shirt and took it off, ignoring the titters and murmurs of the diners around them who were clearly enjoying the show. 'I'll hold this around you while you take your top off, then you can wear it while we free your jumper.'

'Okay,' Jess said, nodding her head unhappily in agreement, managing to look as if he'd just suggested she leap across a pit of poisonous snakes for him.

He looked away as he held his shirt around her so she could struggle out of her jumper without flashing the entire restaurant, then slide her arms into the sleeves. He let go as she pulled it closed around her and attempted to do up the buttons with trembling fingers.

After a couple of frustrating moments of watching her totally fail to do up one single button, he knocked her hands away, knelt down next to the chair and did them up for her.

He could feel her eyes on his face as he worked his way down the shirt, his fingers skirting tantalisingly close to the swell of her breasts.

'Some people would suspect this was a cunning ploy to get me to take my shirt off in public,' he murmured, flipping her a grin, which she returned, albeit humbly. 'There you go.' He stood back so she could get up from the chair.

'Thank you.' She looked really grateful for his help and something lifted in his chest. He quickly released the jumper from the chair back.

'My pleasure. Shall we get out of here, before this crowd asks for an encore?'

'Yes. Good idea,' Jess said, reaching into her hand-bag and grabbing a handful of euros, which she dropped onto the table. He dropped his own share for the meal next to it and handed some of her money back to her. 'You don't need to pay for me.'

She didn't answer, just nodded and gave him a grate-ful smile. He had no idea what she was thinking; from the look in her eyes she seemed to have retreated far away into her own head.

He strode out of the restaurant, aware of the amused glances of the other diners as he passed by them, half-naked and standing out like a sore thumb, with Jess hot on her heels. He gave them all a salute as he reached the door and ushered Jess outside. She ran over to the car and he unlocked the doors so she could get straight in. He swung himself into the driving seat and burst out laughing, turning to look at her and share the joke, but she was staring straight ahead, her back ramrod-straight and her hands clutched tightly in her lap.

'Jess?'

She turned to look at him, her expression wild and her face flaming red. 'Can we go?' It came out as a hushed gasp. She flapped the front of the shirt, clearly trying to cool herself down. He frowned at her extreme reaction. It was warm in the car, but not sweltering.

He started up the engine and drove out of the car park, heading back to the villa. 'You okay?' he asked.

'I'm fine. Just hot. Is it hot in here?' She wafted the shirt forward and back creating a slight draught of air, staring hard at the dashboard.

'Not really.' He put a hand on her arm and felt the

heat of her skin sear through the cotton of the shirt. 'Jess, what's going on?'

She wouldn't look at him. 'I don't like showing people my body. I'm not comfortable with it. Never have been. I get a bit…panicked.'

He frowned, baffled. 'How long have you felt like that?'

She took a deep breath before she answered him. 'Since my early teens. I've struggled with a kind of body dysmorphia and an eating disorder since then. Bulimia.' She screwed up her face in disgust. 'But I haven't let it…you know…get hold of me since my late teens.'

Memories from the last couple of days connected together in his brain like jigsaw pieces. So that explained the baggy, unflattering clothes and her apparent discomfort when eating in front of him.

He leant back in the seat and rubbed a hand over his face. 'I'm surprised.'

'Why?'

'Because you seem so *together*.'

'It's all a front,' she said quietly.

'Takes one to know one,' he murmured to himself.

She didn't seem to have heard him, trapped miles away in her own thoughts.

They reached the villa a minute later and he parked back under the awning and shut off the engine.

He turned to look at her and waited until she looked back at him. 'Well, if it's any consolation, you're easily the most intriguing woman I've met in a long time.'

She snorted, then screwed her eyes shut in embarrassment.

'Mostly because you're smart and funny and passionate,' he said, 'but I wouldn't kick you out of bed either.'

She seemed to swallow hard. 'What?' Her voice was

raspy and appeared to barely make it out of her throat. She stared at him hard, as if she was trying to root out a lie using only the power of her cynicism.

He looked back at her, unblinking. She wouldn't win this one. Mainly because he was telling the truth.

Jess broke eye contact first and he gave himself a mental high five, feeling inordinately pleased with himself, until she turned her head and stared out of the window instead of acknowledging his proposition.

Was she turning him down?

The thought rattled through him like a cold wind. A woman hadn't rejected him like that in a very long time and it didn't feel good.

'Jess?'

She turned back to look at him, her expression confused, but wary, and he instinctively leant forward and cupped the side of her jaw with one hand, his thumb catching against the soft fullness of her bottom lip.

He wanted to kiss her. So badly.

It was an undeniable instinct, driven by a mixture of need and curiosity and a determination to not *allow* her to reject him, and frustration twisted in his gut when he realised she was fighting him and pulling away.

Releasing his grip on her, he reluctantly drew back. 'What's wrong?' he asked, holding up an open-palmed hand.

She opened her mouth, as if to respond, then shook her head hard, her long bob of hair swinging round her face, before reaching for the handle to open the door.

He watched her scramble out of the car, banging her arm on the door in her rush to get away from him.

He slumped back in the chair, staring out into the darkness, hot with anger at himself. What the hell was he thinking, coming on to her like that after what she'd just told him? God, how inappropriate. He needed to straighten himself out—fast. Getting close to Jess was going to take more than chucking a few artless, throw-away platitudes her way before steaming in full force.

He got out of the car and followed her into the villa, a little way behind to give her the space she obviously needed. She turned before she got to the staircase and gave him a strained smile.

'See you tomorrow.' It was a statement, not a ques-tion and he knew for sure there would be no invitation to visit her room that night. Perhaps it was for the best con-sidering how ineptly he seemed to be acting around her.

The best. The best, he chanted inside his head in an attempt to convince himself of it.

'Goodnight, Jess, sleep well,' he called after her, knowing full well a good night's sleep was the last thing *he'd* be getting.

CHAPTER FIVE

JESS COULDN'T SLEEP. Again.

Her body hummed with unsettling sensations after spending the most sexually charged day of her life with the most disquieting man in the world—who she was pretty sure would have kissed her in the car if she hadn't freaked out and run away from him like that. The trouble with being around Xander was that he was such a tactile person she wasn't sure whether she'd read his intentions all wrong. Maybe he meant nothing by it.

The memory of the humiliating *jumper incident* in the restaurant made her whole body flush hot with embarrassment. Xander had been so cool to whip off his own shirt like that to protect her modesty and then she'd been cold and weird with him in the car afterwards.

He must think she was a total loon.

And what the hell had possessed her to tell him about her bulimia? It felt now as if she'd opened up the most delicate part of herself and there was a cold draught blowing in, chilling her to the bone.

Not that he hadn't been sensitive about it. In fact, he'd been lovely about that, too, which only made her want him more.

Because she *did* want him.

More than she'd wanted anyone in her entire life.

And the idea terrified her.

She knew deep in her bones it would be a disaster for her to get emotionally involved with him. He was too wild for her, too... What was the phrase? *Too hot to handle.*

She'd get badly burned; she knew it.

The most sensible thing to do would be to keep it strictly business for the rest of her time here in case she made even more of a fool of herself. But she didn't *want* to be sensible. Not this time.

Trouble was, she had a feeling her stand-offishness was all that separated her from pretty much every other woman he came into contact with and she'd be a fool to squander the advantage of his remarkable interest in her by making herself too available.

All she had to do was keep things in perspective.

Yeah, good luck with that, Jess.

Oh, goodness, this assignment was hard work.

She sighed and rolled over in bed, trying to quell the deep, vigorous throbbing between her legs at the thought of him sleeping just along the corridor.

Impossible.

Perhaps she should go and make herself a milky drink or something, in the hope it would relax her enough to let her sleep.

Rubbing a hand over her tired eyes, she sat up, shuffling to the side of her bed, only managing to increase the ache between her thighs with the friction of the movement.

Never in all her life had she felt so wildly out of control and it scared the hell out of her.

Leaving her room quietly, so as not to disturb Xander, she tiptoed downstairs to the kitchen, leaving off the light in case anyone should be alerted to her presence. She felt furtive and naughty for being there, as if she were trespassing on someone else's property, even though she was a guest in the house.

As she pulled open the fridge door to find the milk her eye was drawn to a bowl of what looked like tiramisu, sitting there innocently in the fridge.

A horrible greedy urge to take it and eat the entire bowlful gripped her around the throat.

The stress of hanging out with Xander Heaton was severely testing her rather shaky self-control.

Her hands shook and her mouth filled with saliva as she stared at the delicious-looking pudding. A tremendously powerful urge to reach forward and take it gripped her, but she knew from experience if she so much as let herself take a mouthful she'd end up stuffing the whole thing into her mouth like some crazed maniac and she really couldn't let that happen. She'd fought so valiantly over the years against the horrible overwhelming feelings of shame and self-loathing her eating disorder prompted, she couldn't let herself get pulled into that vicious cycle of binge and purge again. She'd made a promise to herself not to allow extreme comfort eating to ruin her life any more than it already had.

It would not beat her.

With a determination that she had to pull up from the very depths of her psyche, she swung the fridge door shut and walked away on shaky legs, back to her bedroom and safety.

The next morning Jess got up early and took herself off for a drive around the lake.

She needed a breather from being around Xander in order to mentally get herself in a place where she could handle the developing situation without freaking out again.

A bit of peace and calm and normality was just the ticket.

Stopping off in a few of the charming towns along the way, she took photos and made notes for the travel piece she needed to write. Each place was very different from the last—with its own unique atmosphere and character—all bordering the amazingly clear water of Lake Garda. She could totally see why the place lured so many visitors to its shores each year.

A tantalising window display in one of the women's clothes shops drew her in and she found herself trying on and buying a couple of reasonably priced tops— one white and one in a vibrant pillar-box red—a stylish, black fishtail skirt that fell to just above her knee and a couple of midlength-sleeved summer dresses. All the clothes were more fitted and flamboyant than the things she'd usually wear, but some strange compulsion made her hand over her credit card and buy them anyway. She justified the expense by telling herself she needed some more clothes since it looked as if she was staying longer and it wouldn't be professional to keep turning up in the same sad outfit every day.

After gathering as much information as she needed, she finally made her way back to the villa, feeling drowsy now in the afternoon heat.

As she pulled the car onto the driveway she could see Xander in the distance, a mug of coffee in one hand and a paintbrush in the other, standing in front of an easel set up on the lawn overlooking the lake. He must have heard the car's engine because he turned round to look her way, dropped his paintbrush onto the grass next to a pallet of paints and strode towards her, waving.

'Hey, Jess, there you are.'

He stumbled as he walked towards her, spilling coffee down his trousers.

Jess shot him a grin, glad for the distraction from the anxiety about facing him again after the debacle of the night before.

He raised a questioning eyebrow. 'What's so funny?' he said, brushing at the stain with his fingers.

She shrugged, nerves making her jittery. 'It's nice to see you making mistakes, too. It just proves even the most self-possessed people mess up. I like that—it makes me feel better about myself. If you can spill coffee all over your crotch then it's okay for me to rip my clothes off in a restaurant. Or something.'

He gave her a puzzled look. 'You're a very strange woman, you know that?'

She snorted. 'Actually I do. It's not a new observation.'

He smiled and her blood heated. There was something in his gaze she hadn't seen before. Something that made her insides flip.

'Where have you been today?'

'I went for a drive around the lake. I'm writing a travel piece too while I'm here so I wanted to get a feel of the place.'

'Man, they keep you busy there, don't they?'

She shrugged. 'I like to keep busy.'

He nodded but didn't say anything, his gaze flicking down to her mouth. She tensed under his scrutiny. He seemed to move closer to her, just a fraction, as if he were thinking about going in for a kiss and she froze with anxiety, not at all sure what to do with herself. Her lips tingled at the thought of his mouth, hot and hard against hers.

'I'm a p-professional,' she stuttered in panic and his gaze flicked back to meet hers, amusement clear in his eyes.

'A professional what?' His expression was full of barely contained laugher.

Jess straightened her T-shirt. Smoothed down her hair. 'Here in a professional capacity, I mean, so please don't feel you have to, you know, look after me or anything.'

He nodded a couple of times, still looking at her as if she was the funniest thing he'd ever encountered. 'What if I like looking after you?' His eyes suddenly lit with an idea before she could respond. 'Hey, why don't we bring a picnic down to the cove later? It should be warm enough and if we're lucky we might get a pretty amazing sunset,' he said, cocking his head while he waited for her to agree.

It sounded much too romantic an idea for her liking, but she couldn't spend the next couple of days hiding from him as she had today. She still hadn't got everything she needed in order to write the column and it would be a good opportunity to ask him some more questions while he was relaxed and happy in her company. 'Yeah, sure, that sounds like fun,' she said, not giving her cowardly alter ego a chance to interfere.

'Great. I'll get Rosa to make a hamper up for us. Shall we say eight o'clock again?'

She nodded dumbly. 'Yes. Eight.'

'Okay, then.' He was looking at her so intensely she wondered whether there was something wrong with her face.

'Listen,' he said, finally breaking the silence, 'I hope you didn't think I was being insensitive last night, after we'd talked about your…eating issues.'

He looked genuinely concerned and she felt a rush of affection for him.

'Nah, don't worry about it. I think we were both a bit freaked by what happened in the restaurant. I don't suppose it's often you have to strip off to save your date from dying of embarrassment.'

He laughed. 'As I'm sure you've noticed, I don't have a problem with stripping off.'

Jess felt the inevitable warmth creep up her neck at the thought of his naked, toned torso in such close proximity to her. 'Yeah, well, you don't need to rein that in on my account,' she said, flashing him what she hoped would come across as an affable smile. She wanted to show him she did still have *some* vestige of control in the flirty-banter stakes.

He raised a dark eyebrow and tipped his head in appreciation. 'Noted,' he said, before turning away and walking back to his easel.

Jess paced the floor of the hall, waiting for Xander to turn up and collect her for their picnic tea.

She'd put the pillar-box-red top and pencil skirt on for tonight, then taken the whole ensemble off again. Then a minute later put it back on, telling herself it was a positive step in the right direction to push herself out of her comfort zone.

To *unstuff* herself.

But then again, she needed every ounce of confidence tonight if she was going to get through the evening with her pride intact.

She'd been about to take it off again when she'd caught sight of her wild-eyed reflection in the mirror.

She was turning into a complete loony.

Whatever was happening between her and Xander

was making her lose her mind. She was ninety per cent sure it wasn't all in her head. Okay, maybe eighty, but he'd definitely kicked his flirting up a notch recently.

What the hell was going on? She could have sworn he would have kissed her last night if she hadn't broken the atmosphere by flapping about like a headless chicken. Or was that just a figure of her overactive imagination? In the past she'd been prone to reading more into a situation than was actually there, and it had made her wary about taking anything for granted when it came to men and relationships.

Another thing she hated—making a fool of herself.

Not that she hadn't already managed that in the couple of days she'd been here.

When he finally turned up at five past eight, looking, oh, so divinely edible, she was so nervous the first thing she said was, 'You're late. Again.'

Despite her snippy tone, he gave her an amused grin. 'Are you going to spank me with your ruler, Headmistress? Because I'll take whatever punishment you choose to dish out.'

She took a shaky step back away from him, but kept her gaze locked with his. 'Don't be so facetious,' she murmured, her body tense with the sudden desire to throw herself at him and consequences be damned.

He took a step towards her, closing the gap between them. 'Ooh, yeah, keep using those long words on me, too. I like that.'

She slapped him gently on the arm. 'You're incorrigible.'

He slapped her back, a seductive eyebrow quirked.

Narrowing her eyes in jest, she did it again, feeling the rock-hard muscle of his triceps vibrate under her touch.

Before she could react he wrapped his hand round hers and, trapping it there against him, walked her backwards until her back hit the wall. The heat from his body radiated over her skin, sending zingy electric currents through her limbs.

'This is just like being back in the school playground,' she barely managed to struggle out. Her tongue felt like a lead weight in her mouth and her lips were tight with tension.

He moved his body closer to her and a flood of longing flashed through her. 'Did you like playing kiss chase at school?' he murmured, dipping his head so he could look directly into her eyes. His pupils looked huge against the bright aqua of his irises.

'Of course,' she said, her voice husky and broken. 'And I'm guessing you were always the first kid to suggest playing it?' Staring defiantly back, she attempted to hold her nerve, determined not to be the one to look away first. He was teasing her, trying to trip her up and get her to admit just how much of an effect he had on her. He wasn't going to win, though; she wouldn't let him.

He shifted even closer, bringing with him a waft of his fresh citrus scent.

It was no good—she just wasn't as good at this game as he was. She closed her eyes as an onslaught of lust nearly brought her to her knees.

'Somebody has to take control,' he said quietly.

She glanced up at him, straight into those unfathomable eyes. 'I'd have fought you for it,' she practically whispered, her throat tight with tension.

He smiled in a way that made her whole body ache with longing.

His hand was still trapping hers against his body and

she could feel the faint pulse in his fingertips. Or was that her own pulse that seemed to have taken her over? She throbbed to the beat as it concentrated deep in her pelvis. She was so turned on she felt faintly queasy.

Taking a deep breath, she swivelled to one side so he had to release her from his grip. 'Shall we go?' she said.

His expression flashed with a mixture of surprise and something else. Disappointment?

'Okay, if you like,' he said, his voice rumbling low in his throat. 'I'll grab the food from the kitchen.'

He came back a few moments later with a hamper and a folded square of material, which she assumed was a picnic rug.

Jess reminded herself not to get too excited about how special this all felt. Xander had probably done things like this a million times before with a million other women.

He turned to smile at her. 'Okay, we're set.'

She nodded in agreement and joined him as he walked through the large patio doors, which opened onto the rear garden of the villa, and traversed the path that led down to the cove.

They walked in silence through the muted evening light, Xander cradling the picnic hamper close to his chest. The air was balmy and close with a threatening rainstorm, the atmosphere electric with the promise of a much-needed purge of humidity.

They picked their way over the warm sand of the cove to the far side, just back from the water, where they had a spectacular view of the opposite shore of the lake, which was beginning to glow and twinkle with colourful lights as the sky darkened.

'I hope it doesn't rain on us,' Jess said, gazing at the ominous-looking clouds in the distance.

'We'll be fine for a while,' Xander said, putting down the hamper and flapping open the thick rug, smoothing it carefully flat before gesturing for Jess to sit down on it.

Once she'd made herself comfortable—yanking down hard on her skirt so it covered as much of her legs as possible—he dropped down next to her, so close she could feel the heat of him radiating towards her.

Pulling out cartons of cold meats, salad, olives and a wealth of other local delicacies, he laid them out carefully on the rug and handed her a plate.

'Dig in,' he said, motioning towards the feast in front of them.

While Jess picked out a few things for her plate he reached into the hamper and came out with a couple of oil-fired lamps and lit them with a long match. They cast a soft glow over the area where they sat.

If she hadn't thought it ridiculous she would have assumed he was deliberately setting up a romantic atmosphere. As it was, she was so nervous she could barely eat a thing. Xander didn't remark on it, though; he must have thought talking about food and eating was a no-go area after her confession the night before.

It was kind of him—thoughtful—and she felt a glow of affection towards him.

'You know, you're nothing like I expected you to be.'

He raised a questioning eyebrow. 'No?'

'The press make you out to be some badly behaved lout, but they've clearly got you pegged all wrong.'

He frowned in mock disgruntlement. 'Don't say that. I was rather enjoying living up to my bad-boy reputation.'

She laughed. 'What was it that made you so wild in your youth?' she asked casually, holding her breath as she waited to see whether Xander trusted her enough yet to tell her something that personal about himself.

Those beautiful eyes of his seemed fathomless as he stared at her, his gaze raking her face for signs of... what? A set-up?

Her heart whammed against her chest like a malfunctioning metronome as she waited to see whether he'd answer her question. She needed some interesting backstory to make the story shine, but somewhere in her brain a small voice told her she really wanted to know for herself. She wanted to think the best of him, because despite the arrogance—which she was beginning to suspect was actually a defence mechanism—she really liked him. And not just because he was so gorgeous, but because she sensed there was a whole lot more to him than he ever let anyone else see.

The optimistic side of him must have won because he leant forward, his gaze capturing hers, and said, 'What do you think it was?'

A slow trickle of excitement percolated through her veins as she realised this could be it—he was letting her in. 'Did you have a tough upbringing?' she asked, desperately hoping she hadn't read him all wrong.

He folded his arms across his broad chest, making the muscles in his shoulders and arms bunch beneath his T-shirt. He looked down at the flickering candle between them. 'You could say that. My parents never intended having a child. I was an accident—which my father liked to remind me of every chance he got.' He looked back at her and she was shocked to see insecurity in his expression—something she'd not encountered before. 'My mum died giving birth to me.'

His voice had taken on a steely edge, which sent a shiver of horror through her. 'I paid my way in that family by spending most of my childhood working to keep myself fed and clothed—until my dad kicked me out when I was sixteen. He'd spend most of his time down the pub or the betting office, so I hardly saw him anyway.' He leant back on the rug, anchoring his arms behind him and readjusting his body before looking at her. There was nothing on his face but a blank expression now, as if he'd drawn down the shutters.

'How awful for you.' She could picture him as a child not being allowed to do the things that normal kids did—not being allowed to *be* a child—and it made her chest ache.

He shrugged. 'It was tough at times. I got into a lot of trouble, for shoplifting and fighting and then for my graffiti and got myself a bad reputation. The teachers wrote me off after a few years of failing to straighten me out.'

She'd known children like that when she was at school. Loners. Lost souls. People who had difficulty fitting into what everyone else thought of as normal life because they'd never had the opportunity to experience it.

The atmosphere had dropped dark now and she wanted to pull it back before the hard pressure behind her eyes became real tears for him.

'But look at you now.' She managed to catch the wobble at the end of the sentence and turn it into a gentle clearing of her throat. 'Everyone wants to own a piece of the great and talented Xander Heaton,' she finished on a deeply concentrated frown as she battled to conceal her need to jump into his lap and rub herself all over him.

'And which piece are you after, Jess?' he asked, leaning forward now and giving her a seductive grin, the heavy atmosphere of the last couple of minutes evaporating into the air around them.

He was king of the suggestive comment, this guy.

All she could think about now was exactly which bits of Xander she'd like to get her hands on. Her mind flew to an image of his magnificent body, prostrate on her bed, with him wearing only a sheet and that mesmerising smile. She pictured herself leaning over him, lowering her lips to his as she attempted to kiss away all the pain that kept him so distant from the rest of the world....

'Jess?' He was frowning at her now as if he was afraid she'd walked through a door marked 'crazy' and wasn't coming back.

'Yeah?' She slid her hands over her hair in an attempt to straighten herself out. Neat hair, neat mind.

'You okay?'

'Fine.' She stared out across the lake, attempting to bring herself back to reality.

'Did you go to college or university to study art?' she asked to fill the uncomfortable silence.

Putting his plate down, he leant back on his arms and looked out across the water. 'Nah, I'm mostly self-taught. I left school when I left home at sixteen without any qualifications so no college would have touched me with a bargepole. I messed up a lot at school because of having to work late into the evening and being too tired to concentrate. Then I started skipping a lot because I couldn't keep up with the lessons and ended up feeling stupid, and I *hated* that. So when I left I didn't exactly have a bright and shiny future ahead of me.

'Art was the only subject I enjoyed at school. It was the one thing I felt I was actually good at, and I had an amazing teacher who really encouraged me. Unfortunately I wasn't in the right mindset at that age to put enough work into my lessons—I didn't think for a second I could make any money out of it, and that's all that concerned me at the time—so it just became a hobby. After I left school, I used to go out in the dead of night with a crew and paint or spray the walls of public buildings with my pictures as a kind of release from the boredom of my existence. Art helped me channel the rage I felt that I didn't feel able to express in words.'

Jess experienced a swell of outrage for him. 'I can't believe no one at the school realised you needed more help and support.'

'Yeah, well, it was an underprivileged area and there were other kids a lot worse off than me. And to be honest, I wasn't interested in their help. I wanted to prove to myself I could manage on my own.'

Jess thought about her own cushy upbringing. Despite the feeling of never managing to become the daughter her mother wanted, she'd never had to worry about coping without enough food or sleep.

Shame washed over her in a hot wave, prickling at her skin, as she realised she'd allowed herself to prejudge Xander, before finding out the reasons for him acting the way he did. It wasn't because he got off on it and enjoyed the notoriety—although that obviously played a small part—it was because he was trying to live his life at triple the speed to make up for what he'd lost in the past.

She couldn't fault him for that.

'You're incredible,' she blurted. 'Look at what you've done with your life. You've made it count with no support and no qualifications.'

'Yeah, well, I'm stubborn like that,' he said on a smile.

'It's impressive.'

'Thanks.' He readjusted his position on the rug, drawing his body closer to her.

An intense longing shot through her, taking her right to the edge of her comfort zone. If she'd thought she'd wanted him before, it was nothing to how much she wanted him now. These insights into his character both fascinated and terrified her—she could totally see why he kept himself so emotionally distant from his partners—but did that mean he'd never be able to settle down with one person?

From what he'd said the night before, it certainly sounded as if *he'd* decided that was the case.

But was there scope to change his mind?

Don't even think about it, Jess.

'What did your father say when you became so successful?' she asked, trying to steer her thoughts back to safer ground. 'He must have been proud of you for what you've achieved?'

Xander barked out a harsh laugh, making her jump. 'Are you kidding? He never turned up to see any of the stuff I've showcased. He thought art was a waste of time. He thought *I* was a waste of time.'

'So you never reconciled things with him? Even after you left home and made it big?'

'You could say that. The last time we laid eyes on each other he told me he wished I hadn't been born because then my mother would still be alive.'

'Oh, my God, Xander, that's awful.'

He shrugged, clearly going for cool nonchalance, but as she continued to look at him he turned away so she couldn't see his face any more.

'But he raised you. He must have cared about you in some way,' she said, quietly.

'It was a long time ago, Jess. I barely even think about it any more.'

He was lying; she could tell. It was obvious from the clip in his voice and the way his body had become rigid with tension.

She put a hand on his arm but he pulled it away and threw his plate back into the hamper.

'Is this the kind of thing you're after to impress your editor?' he asked, his voice tinged with scorn.

Clearly she'd hit a nerve.

She shook her head quickly. 'I want to try and understand what it is that drives you, to round the piece out and give a fair and honest representation of you as a person.'

'Am I not interesting enough to write about without you feeling the need to expose my deepest, darkest secrets?'

'Of course you are.'

Tears welled in her eyes and a thud of shame landed in her stomach as he turned back and she saw pain and disappointment in his expression.

'I won't write about any of that, I promise. I'm sorry for prying. It wasn't to get some salacious gossip out of you; I was genuinely concerned.'

'Well, you don't need to be. I've coped fine without your pity up until this point.'

They gazed at each other in silence for a moment, before Xander turned away to look back out across the lake.

Now she was beginning to see the real Xander she felt a desperate urge to keep that side of him as protected as he did, to keep that side of him just for her.

What was happening to her? She'd been so determined not to fall for his charms when she first arrived here and now all she could think about was how to get closer to him, even though she knew there was little chance he'd ever be interested in a real relationship with her.

How could she want someone and some*thing* that terrified her so much?

She picked at her food some more, eventually laying the plate down on the rug in front of her in defeat. It had been delicious, but she just couldn't bring herself to eat any more of it, not when her stomach felt as if it were full of rolling marbles.

'You had enough?' he asked, nodding at her abandoned plate.

'Er, yeah.' She was glad he couldn't see how flushed her face was in the growing darkness.

After packing the remainder of the food back into the hamper in silence, he lay down on the rug and gazed up at the sky.

Jess couldn't stop looking at him, thinking about how his powerful body would feel under her hands and how overwhelmed by his enigmatic presence she was, despite her determination to keep herself emotionally distant. He did something to her she couldn't explain.

Turning his head, he caught her gawping at him.

'Sorry for flipping out like that. Don't take it personally—I'm just in a bit of a funk today,' he said.

Shaking herself out of her trance, she fumbled around for the wherewithal to get herself back under control.

'I can understand why you don't feel comfortable talking to journalists about your past. It must have been really hard growing up like that.'

He sat up, turning to fully face her and brushing his hands together before carefully laying them on his lap. 'Yeah, well, in my experience some journalists make it their life's work to root out your most embarrassing secrets just to sell a few papers and get their byline next to the story.'

'You have some *embarrassing* secrets? Can you tell me about *those* so I can cash in and make my fortune?' she said, willing a gleam of mischief into her expression.

He raised an eyebrow at her, but smiled. 'I'll tell you mine if you tell me yours,' he said, leaning forward so their eyes were on a level.

The smile dropped from her face as she struggled to deal with his sudden closeness. That feeling was back, the one from earlier, when she'd thought he was going to kiss her.

His gaze flicked from her eyes to her mouth and the surge of need to be kissed nearly made her crumple in a heap. She throbbed with it.

As if sensing her desperate want, he leant in farther, his seductive gaze locked with hers, closing the distance between them.

Her breath came shallow and fast from her lungs and her heart raced in her chest as his mouth came so close to hers she could feel the whisper of his breath on her lips.

She was frozen. Captivated. Caught. She dared not move a muscle in case she turned to dust in front of him.

'What do you want from me, Jess?' he murmured against her mouth so she felt the vibration of the sound on her skin and right down to her toes.

Closing her eyes, she grasped for a thin thread of courage to say what she wanted out loud, but the words wouldn't come. They were stuck hard in the back of her throat.

Say it, Jess. Stop being such a coward and say it.

'I want to touch you,' she whispered. 'I want to know what your body feels like.'

Opening her eyes, she saw he was looking at her intently. There wasn't a trace of the condescension she'd expected to see, only acceptance and approval.

'Go ahead.' He drew back quickly from her, leaving a chasm of cool air where he'd once been and tugged his shirt over his head, revealing his amazing body.

Taking a deep, shaking breath, she stared at him in shock for a moment, her brain taking a second to catch up with the sudden and stupefying turn of events. Had he really just offered up his body for her to fondle?

Please let it be so.

'Go on,' he urged, taking one of her trembling hands in his and placing it against his warm chest.

His skin almost glowed in the lamplight, and it felt as soft as she'd imagined, more so if that was possible, and the hard muscle underneath moved gently under her touch as he readjusted his position.

Putting his hand over the back of hers, he lay back on the rug, pulling her with him so she had to kneel up and lean over him.

He nodded at her as if urging her on and she slowly moved her hand down his chest to the top of his stomach where the muscles swelled against his skin like perfectly formed moguls.

'Is it everything you expected?' he murmured, giving her a slow smile that made the blood rush and fizz between her legs.

'Uh-huh,' was all she managed as her whole body shook with the effort of not collapsing against him.

'Okay, my turn.'

Before she knew what was happening, he sat up, grasping her shoulders and flipping her onto her back underneath him, trapping her legs between his knees and her wrists in his hands.

'Just say the word, Jess, and I'll let you go.' He leant in closer. 'But please don't,' he begged. 'I think I'm going to go crazy if I don't get to touch you.'

She just stared up at him, befuddled and entranced by the fact that *she had the ability to drive him crazy.*

Had the world gone mad? Since when did she get to hold the cards with a man like this?

Since now, Jess.

He took her silence as consent and released her wrists so he could use his hands to stroke along the tops of her shoulders, before sweeping down and pushing up the sleeves of her top to uncover her arms.

It had been such a long time since she'd been touched like this that her body nearly melted with joy.

His touch was feather-light and slow, his fingertips sweeping over every inch of her bare arms, tracing the lines between her muscles and pausing on one of the many dark moles on her skin.

'I love this mole here,' he said, quietly. 'It's such a perfectly round shape. Beautiful.' Moving on down her arms, he dipped his fingers into the well of her inner elbows. 'Your skin is so soft,' he said, swirling the pads of his fingers around the sensitive skin there until she thought she'd go crazy with it.

'You have an amazing body, Jess,' he said, his gaze moving down to take in the swell of her breasts as they pushed against her new—lucky—red top. 'I've been thinking about it all day.'

Had he *really*?

Shuffling down her body, he moved one of his knees to release her legs, pushing it instead between her thighs to open her up to him.

Her heart raged in her chest as she realised what he was about to do, his hand dipping down to caress the soft skin of her inner thigh that her skirt didn't cover.

'Wait,' she whispered so quietly he couldn't have heard her.

Both of his hands were between her legs now, making gentle stroking sweeps up from her knees to the soft plumpness of her inner thighs, his thumbs drawing erotic figures of eight across her flesh.

Great crashing waves of need flowed over her, making the space between her legs ache and pulse with the demand to be touched.

Any second now, he'd move higher, to the line of her knickers, then higher… The thought brought her crashing back down to earth.

'No.' Her voice was loud this time, loud enough to make him pause in what he was doing.

'Jess?' His own voice was ragged and low and not at all steady. 'What's wrong?'

Shuffling back away from his touch, she pulled her skirt down hard to her knees before scrambling to get up. Her legs were like jelly as she backed away from him, stumbling on the uneven ground.

'Jess? Where are you going?' His voice was filled with genuine shock and concern.

'I have to… I need to…' She couldn't form the words. They wouldn't come. She had to get out of there but she couldn't tell him why. She just couldn't. It was too humiliating.

Xander stared after Jess's retreating figure until she was swallowed up by the darkness.

He'd never been so frustrated in his life. His hands shook with the need to touch her again and the hard press of his erection against his trousers was almost painful.

He'd thought he was starting to get through to her, to help her realise just how sexy and attractive she really was, but she'd thrown up her wall again and he'd run right into it.

Goddamn it.

Perhaps he'd pushed her too hard too soon? But he couldn't see how that could be the case. He'd been taking it *way* slower than he wanted to and she'd been there with him right up until the end.

The eating disorder had obviously had a huge psychological effect on the way she saw her own body, because from what he'd seen she had a fantastic figure, all soft curves in the right places but toned and sculpted from regular exercise. Out of bounds, though, obviously.

He knew he should leave it at that. He shouldn't be doing this with someone like Jess when he had nothing more than his body to offer her, but he couldn't stop himself. Didn't want to. He felt some deep connection with her that he'd never experienced with anyone before and he wanted to explore it more. Despite her reluctance.

Was she afraid of what was happening between them and protecting herself? He couldn't blame her; he didn't exactly have a great reputation when it came to women and relationships.

But Jess wasn't like the other women he'd dated.

This felt more special, more real. Partly because he was having to work hard to get her to trust him, but also because he wanted her to understand where he came from.

He wanted her approval.

And he wanted to go after her—like nothing he'd

ever wanted before. He sensed she was worried about what was happening between them and he wanted to reassure her that there was nothing to be afraid of.

Jumping up, he pulled his shirt back on before heading off in the direction she'd disappeared.

There was no way in *hell* he was giving up on her now.

CHAPTER SIX

SHE WAS SUCH a coward.

Jess slammed the door to her room hard in frustration. What the hell was she doing running away from Xander like that?

Truth was, she'd never had a one-night stand in her life and the thought of it petrified her. Especially with someone as *intensely male* as him.

She was scared of not being able to give him what he expected from her.

He must be used to bedding sexually confident women with their lithe, toned bodies and dexterity in the bedroom and he was going to be mightily disappointed when he found out how useless she was in bed.

A loud knock at the door made her jump in fright.

That couldn't be him, could it? Surely he'd realised by now she wasn't the type of woman he should be wasting his time with? He'd given her so many opportunities to take him up on his sexual invitations and she'd blown every one of them. He must be mightily bored with her inability to take the initiative by now.

She paused on the way to answer the door as an uncomfortable notion struck her. Perhaps he thought she was playing hard to get?

Had she really given him that impression?

She thought back to all the teasing and flirting she'd allowed herself to indulge in over the last couple of days.

Yup, she probably had.

Swinging the door open, she found him standing there with his thumbs casually hooked into the belt loops of his jeans, like some vision from an advert for sex. Pushing her shoulders back, she attempted to convey cool control, all the while shaking in her shoes.

'What do you want?' she asked, her voice low and husky with nerves.

'I want *you*,' he said quietly and she sucked in a sharp breath as he suddenly advanced towards her, placing a hand each side of her jaw and pulling her towards him, his mouth pressing hard against hers before she could stop him.

His lips crushed her mouth, soft, yet hard with hunger as he forced her lips open so he could slide his tongue between them. He tasted delicious, like the most delectable main course and the sweetest dessert all wrapped up in one sensational feast.

Sliding his hands under her buttocks, he lifted her up against him and she felt the rigid length of his erection press against the agonisingly sensitised nerves between her legs.

She groaned low in her throat as he slammed her against the wall and pushed against her, increasing the delicious friction between their bodies.

'I want you like this, Jess, just like this, fast and hard against the wall,' he murmured against her mouth, his fingers slipping into her hair, holding her captive. 'Then afterwards, slow and long…sliding into you over and over again.'

She nearly stopped breathing as the sound of those

words washed over her, drenching her to her quivering bones. But she couldn't let him expect that might happen.

She *couldn't.*

Putting both hands against his shoulders, she pushed him away from her hard.

He stumbled back, catching himself before he fell against the bed and staring at her with a bewildered expression.

She wanted to cry.

'I'm sorry,' she said. 'I'm so sorry.'

'Jess, what is it?' Xander took a step towards her but stopped his advance when she shrank against the wall.

'I...don't want to disappoint you,' she said so quietly he almost missed it.

He stared at her, baffled. 'You won't.'

Moving towards her again, slowly this time, he wrapped his hands around her upper arms and manoeuvred her over to the bed, pushing her down gently to sit on it and kneeling in front of her between her thighs.

Their eyes were on a level and she gazed into his as he drew closer to her, their lips only centimetres apart.

'This is just another barrier you're throwing up.' He put a hand under her chin and forced her to look at him. 'I know you want me, Jess. I can see it in your eyes.'

She stared at him, her eyes wild. 'I don't think it's a good idea, Xander.'

He snorted and pushed himself up to standing, moving away from her. He'd never met anyone so wary about sleeping with him. Perhaps his damn reputation was getting in the way here? She seemed pretty hung up on how he ran his sex life.

'Are you scared of me?'

The question seemed to shock her. Scrambling backwards onto the bed, she curled her arms around her drawn-up legs, staring at him, frowning hard. 'Of course I'm not scared of you.'

'Then what is it?'

'I just don't need any more complications in my life right now.'

'Why does this need to be complicated?'

'I'm not the sort of person that sleeps around for fun, Xander. It's not my thing.'

'How can having a night of hot, meaningless sex with me not be your "thing"?' he said. 'It seems to me you're severely lacking *something*, because you're clearly not happy.'

She frowned hard. 'I don't need sex to be happy.'

He threw her a scathing look.

'I don't,' she said, giving herself away with the wobble in her voice.

'So you're totally fine without any affection, are you? Without allowing yourself the odd night of crazy, random fun, just for the hell of it?'

'Yes.' She tried to push her shoulders back and give it some front but she was obviously too tense to make it work and sank back into her crouch again.

She looked younger, smaller and more vulnerable like that and a sudden raging need to protect her came out of left field. He sat back down on the end of the bed so he wasn't towering above her any more.

'Why did you say you're worried about disappointing me?'

She huffed out a sigh and shook her head. 'Come on, Xander, you know what I'm talking about.'

Twisting onto his knees, he moved up the bed and

slid into the space next to her, close enough to smell the heady scent of her perfume.

'I'm not even *remotely* like the women you usually date.'

'Perhaps that's why I like you so much.'

'You *like* me?'

'Believe it or not, I like your company. You're the most genuine, interesting, *surprising* person I've met in a long time. And correct me if I'm wrong, but I think you've got a thing for me, too, despite your misgivings,' he said, flashing her a grin. He was being totally honest with her here and he hoped to God he hadn't read the situation wrong.

He really wanted this thing between them to grow and develop. She was all he could think about at the moment and he wanted her. Badly.

The corner of her mouth twitched up into a smile. 'Okay, I admit, I like being around you. You can be good fun when you're not trying to trip me up with your *massive ego.*'

The little minx.

Before she could react, he moved towards her, pulling her arms from around her body and hooking one knee over her legs, while simultaneously trapping her wrists against the bed behind her—imprisoning her beneath him.

'Maybe you should let go of that disabling control and do something crazy for once. Just for the hell of it,' he murmured, gazing down at those captivating eyes of hers as he dipped his mouth towards her.

'Wait. Xander.'

He paused midway to her lips and waited for her to finish her sentence, feeling her breath hot and sweet on his skin.

She screwed up her eyes, as if she had to pretend he wasn't there in order to get the words out. 'I don't find it easy to orgasm. I'm too self-aware.' Her cheeks flushed with mortification. 'I'm useless in bed. That's why I'll disappoint you.'

When she opened her eyes, all he could do was stare at her in disbelief. 'Who on earth told you that?'

She looked up at him, barely able to meet his gaze. 'The last guy I had a relationship with. But I've always been unsure of myself where sex is concerned,' she rushed on. 'I don't exactly have a lot of experience.' She looked away from him again, her face pale now.

He stared at her in silence for a moment, feeling inexplicably angry. 'What a jerk.' No wonder she was so afraid of letting him get physical with her. Who said things like that to someone they were meant to care about? Even though he'd never allowed himself to get emotionally close to any of the women he'd slept with, he'd never dream of being so callous and cruel to them. The guy clearly hadn't bothered to get to know Jess very well if he couldn't see how saying something like that to her would destroy her fragile confidence.

'I guess my inability to enjoy sex with him must have fed into his deepest insecurities about not being man enough or something,' she said, looking at him now with shame in her eyes.

'Clearly he *wasn't* man enough.'

She gave him a tentative smile back and something tightened in his chest.

'Yeah. Maybe.'

'Jess, listen, I hear what you're saying, but I don't want to walk away now, leaving you believing you'll never enjoy or be good at sex. Give me the opportunity to change your mind.'

He wanted to give her this—a chance to step out from behind that cloud of doubt that followed her around and to feel the sunshine on her face for once. He knew his strengths and weaknesses, and while he couldn't offer her a hearts-and-flowers relationship, he was more than qualified to show her a good time in the sack.

'You like a challenge, don't you?' she said, the corner of her mouth twitching.

He put a hand up to her face and stroked her cheek with the backs of his fingers.

'Trust me, Jess, you won't regret it.'

Jess stared at him and thought about how much she wanted to let herself have him—have this—and how she needed to start taking risks in her life if she was ever going to start really *living*.

'Tonight doesn't have to mean anything, Jess. Just think of it as a blip in the timeline. A chance to step out of yourself for a few hours. You can button yourself right back up again afterwards if you want.' He shot her a playful grin. 'Give me the chance to prove to you that sex can be more fun than you think.'

Her blood pulsed hard through her veins, the crazy adrenaline rush making her head spin. There was a good chance she'd go loopy if she didn't let this happen. The regret would stay with her till her dying day.

After all, she'd come here determined to get some new experiences out of the trip and he was offering her something incredible—a no-strings night and his heavenly body on a plate.

Her deeply ingrained insecurities waged war with her libido.

She wanted to, but the thought of him seeing her naked terrified her.

'You can't take all my clothes off and it has to be dark,' she stated, wondering if she was pushing things a bit too far. Surely he'd get fed up with it all soon and get up and leave. That was what most men would do.

But Xander wasn't most men.

He raised an eyebrow. 'You're determined to throw every single obstacle in my way, aren't you?' Lifting a hand, he trapped a curl of her hair between his fingers and gave it a gentle tug before wrapping it around her ear. 'It's a good job I relish a challenge.'

He leant across and turned off the lamp next to the bed, plunging the room into darkness.

He wasn't giving her any time to back out.

She felt him shift his position on the bed next to her and wished for a second she hadn't insisted on turning off the light. Suddenly a layer of control had gone. If she couldn't see him, she couldn't pre-empt what he was going to do and stop him.

Man, she was strung out. There was no way he was getting an orgasm out of her tonight. The thought made her even more tense. A vicious circle.

He obviously sensed her growing panic because he laid a hand gently on her foot. 'Jess. Relax. It's going to be okay.' Xander's words twisted through her head and she clung onto the sound of his voice to steady herself.

Pushing herself up onto her elbows, she tried to locate him in the gloom. She could make out the general shape of him, but no details. 'I apologise in advance if it takes me a while to…you know,' she said quickly, before the insecurity won and muted her.

'Don't worry, we have all night.' Her whole body responded to his seductive tone with an intense shiver from her ears right down to her toes. 'Trust me, okay? Just trust me. This is about *you* tonight. I don't want you to worry about me. I want to do this for you. I'm going to enjoy it.'

Oh. My. God.

'Lie back,' he said, skating his hands gently, oh, so gently, up her thighs.

It would be so much easier if she just got up and left right now, but she couldn't do it. Didn't want to. Wouldn't let herself. Not this time.

He had her pinned there with the sheer force of his magnetism.

Moving his hands slowly under her skirt to the apex of her thighs, testing her reaction inch by inch, he eventually encountered her knickers.

Biting down on her lip to stop herself from asking him to stop, Jess allowed him to slide his thumbs inside the leg holes, close, so close to where her body throbbed and buzzed with the heat he'd continually triggered in her ever since she'd arrived here.

Closing her eyes, she raised her hips and let him slide her knickers down her legs, feeling the pads of his fingers trail from the tops of her thighs, right down to her ankles, his touch leaving a burning trail along her skin.

Sucking in a breath, she waited—the anticipation of his next move making her blood pulse hot and fast through her body.

'Tell me what you like, Jess. Where you want to be touched.' His voice rumbled through her.

'I don't know. I don't know what I like,' she whispered, so glad he couldn't see how hard she was blushing. She was amazed he hadn't commented on how hot it was in the room—how she seemed to be giving off more heat than the national grid.

'Okay, let's experiment. You tell me when I'm hitting the right spots.'

Before she had chance to process what he'd said, she felt a movement of air on her legs and the bed dipped underneath her. A second later, his breath tickled the now hypersensitive skin of her inner thigh before he dropped his head to kiss her there, right below the juncture of her thighs.

She jumped in shock at the intimacy of it all, struggling for a second with the realisation of exactly what he was about to do to her. He didn't comment on her reaction, just moved his kisses lower, down towards her knees, as if he realised he'd gone in a bit too hot and heavy. He was reading her body like a pro, shifting his position and the intensity of his kisses depending on how she reacted. He spent a while working his way from the tips of her toes right back to the tops of her thighs, his slow exploration ratcheting up her need to be touched in a way she had no words to describe. They wouldn't come, refusing to allow her to ask for the pleasure she craved.

Seeming to sense her struggle with herself, Xander finally moved higher, between her thighs, then higher again, slowly and so gently, until he hovered over where she ached to be touched, his breath tickling her, teasing her.

He was waiting for her to say the words, to give him permission.

Gripping the bedspread hard between her hands for courage, she screwed up her eyes in concentration and forced the words to leave her throat. 'There. Just there. Yes.' She sounded so guttural, so desperate, it shocked her.

Her reward for finally allowing the words to come

was worth every ounce of effort. He stroked his tongue gently over her and she responded without thinking, raising her pelvis off the bed and pressing herself into him. Clearly taking that as a positive response, he spread his fingers against her thighs, pushing them wider—a gentle flow of movement that made her whole body throb and ache.

He dipped his head to her again and kissed her there hard. 'I love your body, you smell so good, taste so good,' he murmured against the sensitive nub of her clitoris, the vibration upping the intensity of the feeling.

Oh, he *so* knew what he was doing.

He worked his tongue against her, taking long leisurely sweeps, only touching her directly there for a second before moving on.

It was torture. Sweet torture.

Moving his hands up her body, he found the hem of her top and slid his fingers beneath it, finding the hot skin of her stomach. She sucked it in quickly, distracted from the roving path of his tongue for a second.

He sensed her withdrawal and removed his hand, placing it instead under her buttocks, pushing her upwards, harder against his mouth until she forgot all about her insecurities again.

Her breath tore against her throat and she gasped as each stroke of his tongue took her closer, closer than she'd ever been before to an orgasm with someone else.

But she needed more. *Something* more.

As if sensing her hesitation, Xander pulled away from her and she felt him shuffle his way carefully up her body until his dark shadow loomed above her.

'You are easily the sexiest woman I've ever met,' he said in such a guttural voice she felt a jubilant thrill deep in her chest. 'I love how you respond so honestly to me, even when you don't know you're doing it.'

Dropping his head slowly until he found her mouth in the dark, he kissed her gently, skimming his tongue across her lower lip. Moving a hand back between her thighs, he slid his fingers over her swollen folds, parting her there before sliding downwards slowly, so excruciatingly slowly. She gasped against his mouth as his fingers penetrated her, delving deep inside, opening her up to him.

A groan escaped from low in her throat and she instinctively opened her legs wider to give him better access.

His fingers slid deeper, the silkiness of her arousal allowing him easy access, and he pulsed them inside her, finding a spot that made her jump and twist with pleasure when he pressed hard.

Slicking his thumb against her clitoris, he kept up the pressure of his touch, and she moved, unthinking, against it, forcing herself to relax into the moment and just feel.

She wanted to be able to do this. So much. And Xander didn't seem at all concerned about how long it was taking her to get there.

Turning her thoughts away from anything but how he was making her crazy with only the amazing dexterity of those beautiful hands of his, she rode the movement with him, breathing in the enticing tang of his scent as he hovered his mouth above hers, the intensity of it all making her head spin.

Focus, Jess, focus on the pleasure. Find the joy.

As she relaxed into the rhythm of their movement she became aware of a concentrated pressure building inside her where his fingers twisted and pulsed. It started as a slow tingle, steadily growing into a great throbbing spasm, which intensified second after second, keeping her on the edge of reaching something amazing, for what felt like *for ever*.

'Let go, Jess,' Xander whispered against her mouth, the words vibrating on her lips, and suddenly, without warning, the feeling seemed to break and implode inside her, the rush of intensity taking her breath away.

'Whoa…whoa…*whoa*!' She writhed and twitched in ecstasy, completely out of control of her body's movements as a great thundering orgasm twisted through her, emanating from deep inside and radiating out until she felt it to the tips of her fingers. Blood roared through her head, and exquisite pleasure chased around her body as wave after wave of intense sensation flowed through her.

It took her a while to return to reality as she lived through the aftershocks her body seemed intent on throwing at her.

Xander hadn't moved, but now she felt him lean across her, his hard body pressing against the tips of her breasts, his breath tickling her ear. There was a click next to her head and the bedside light flickered on.

He hovered above her with the smuggest smile she'd ever encountered splashed across his handsome face.

She stared up at him in incredulity. 'What did you *do* to me?'

'I found your G spot.' He flopped onto the bed next to her.

'Wow. I've never come like that before,' she said, sitting up and pulling her skirt back down, smoothing her hands over it to flatten it out. She was finding it hard to look at him. All her barriers had been smashed to smithereens and she didn't know how she was supposed to act any more.

'Well, congratulations,' he murmured. Leaning forward, he put a hand to her chin and tipped her face towards him. Quickly closing the gap between them, he kissed her gently on the lips. 'It just takes a bit of patience. I'm guessing the men you've slept with in the past were more interested in their own pleasure than yours.'

She thought back to the last guy she'd slept with. She hadn't liked the way he'd touched her, all urgent and hard, as if he'd wanted to get her pleasure out of the way quickly so he could focus on his own.

'You could say that,' she said. 'The last sexual relationship I had started off as uninspiring and went downhill from there. I ended up faking my orgasms just to get it over with so he'd leave me alone.' Pulling her legs towards her chest, she wrapped her arms around her knees and hugged her legs tightly against her body.

It had been easier to lie to the guy, but she'd felt disappointed and angry with herself afterwards. She knew it was a psychological block she had about relaxing enough to let her body respond how it should and she'd reconciled herself to the belief that she'd never be able to let herself go enough.

Until Xander came along with his dogged determination.

How completely and utterly bizarre the whole situation was. It was as if she'd just tumbled down the rabbit hole and found herself in a new, completely baffling world.

Her expression must have reflected some of her bewilderment because Xander frowned and put a hand on her shoulder. 'Are you okay?'

His show of concern made her chest constrict. He seemed to be genuinely worried about how she was handling it all.

She gave him a smile, which she hoped transmitted more poise than she felt right at that moment. 'I'm fine. Thanks.'

He grinned. 'So it *is* possible for you to orgasm with someone else in the room.'

She snorted and shook her head in amusement at his awe-inspiring confidence. 'Yeah, okay, you were right, apparently you *are* a sex magician.'

'A sex magician.' He smiled. 'I like the way your mind works, Jess.'

She felt light-headed and discombobulated by it all— and suddenly, overwhelmingly tired. A yawn pushed against the back of her throat and she tried in vain to suppress it.

Xander grinned in amusement. 'Okay, I'm going to let you sleep now.'

Before she could say anything he rolled away from her, off the bed and onto his feet in one fluid movement.

'See you in the morning, Jess.' He blew her a kiss. 'Sweet dreams.'

She watched his retreating figure until he'd pulled open the door and disappeared through it, letting it click closed behind him.

She wasn't sure whether to laugh or cry.

Her whole world had been tipped upside down and she felt suddenly very lost and alone and horrifically guilty about not giving him any pleasure back.

No wonder he'd got up and left.

And she didn't know what to do next.

Now she'd allowed her hard-clung-to control to slip

she was in some kind of crazy limbo, not sure which way to turn.

Xander had made it pretty clear he was all about the here and now and that tonight was just a bit of fun for him and she didn't know what to think about that. On the one hand she didn't want that to be it for them— now she'd toppled over the line she wanted more time to explore this brave new world with him—but on the other, she had a horrible feeling she wouldn't be able to be as casual about sex with Xander as he apparently could be with her.

Could she risk it?

If she decided to walk away now and keep her sanity—and quite possibly her heart—intact, she'd need to go first thing in the morning, before things became awkward and uncomfortable for them both.

But could she bring herself to do that?

Based on his reputation she'd be a fool to think anything long-term could come out of this, but, damn it, she couldn't just walk away now, leaving things hanging between them.

She wanted more.

Flopping back onto the pillows, she rubbed a hand over her drowsy eyes.

Sleep, that was what she needed right now. The crazy whirl of emotions had exhausted her and she could barely think straight any more.

Yes, sleep now.

There would be time for decisions in the morning.

Xander paced around his bedroom, weirdly adrenalised from the effort of walking away from Jess when all he'd wanted to do was bury himself inside her and stay there all night.

To lose himself in her.

Giving his face a vigorous rub to get the blood flowing, he stared at his eyes in the mirror and tried to pull himself together.

He'd never done that before—put someone else's needs before his own—and he was amazed by just how fantastic it felt. He was making a positive difference to her life, helping her find something she'd been missing for too long, and the thought of it warmed him.

Xander Heaton, Sex Therapist. Who'd have thought it possible?

It had been hell on earth to walk away, but he was glad he'd done it. He could see they needed to take things slowly so she could keep some vestige of control. Judging by the way she'd closed herself up again afterwards, she evidently needed space away from him now.

So did he if he was honest.

He couldn't put his finger on exactly why he felt so unsettled by what had just happened between them, but it unnerved him something crazy.

Perhaps it was because he liked her so much. The lovers he'd had in the past had been very sexy, engaging women, but he'd never enjoyed being with them the way he enjoyed being around Jess. There were so many layers to her that he got the feeling he might never get to the heart of who she was.

She fascinated him.

And he was having *fun*. He seemed able to push away the anxiety that had plagued him for the last year when she was around.

She calmed him—and he needed that right now. It would be good for him to have her company here while he worked on his exhibition.

He just needed to find a way to persuade her to stay.

CHAPTER SEVEN

JESS SLEPT BADLY, despite her exhaustion, trying like mad to put the thought of what had happened with Xander out of her mind until the morning.

She failed spectacularly, of course. He was all she could think about.

He'd made her feel like the most important, fascinating, *sexy* woman on earth for those few short hours and she knew she wanted that feeling back, *so desperately.* She could almost taste the tang of need like a physical reaction in her taste buds.

The fact he'd seemed to genuinely find her a turn-on had helped something begin to shift in her head. It wasn't as though she suddenly felt like throwing off all her clothes and running around in the nude, but his gentle attentions and the stream of compliments had made her start to think about her body in a different way.

Rolling out of bed, she walked over to the cheval mirror in the corner and stood naked in front of it. For the first time in a very long time she looked at herself—*really* looked—studying the places he'd mentioned he liked so much, running her fingers over the dips and swells of her figure and tracing the lines of the muscles that delineated her body.

She was surprised by how different she felt this

morning, after finally allowing herself to release the brakes on her control and discovering that the earth hadn't crashed around her ears. It was as if she'd uncovered something new and secret and hidden about herself, after all these years.

Something that Xander had seen all along.

After showering, she dressed quickly, her body humming with a strange excitement.

She needed to see Xander, if for no other reason than to prove to herself he was real and she hadn't just dreamt it all up.

He was in his studio, stripped to the waist and engrossed in what he was painting on a large canvas. There was a dark smudge of paint on his left cheek, as if he'd absent-mindedly swiped at his face with dirty hands as a child would.

There was something so pure and human about that, something that made her chest contract with acute sadness for him. He was alone in the world and carrying around such a heavy load of pain and anger it made her want to cry. No wonder he couldn't settle down if he'd never known what it felt like to be loved. She so desperately wanted to show him how it could feel, but she was terrified she wasn't strong enough or bright enough or alive enough to get through to him.

Was she brave enough to at least give it a try?

She still hadn't figured out what she was going to write about him for the magazine. That really ought to be her top priority, *not* working out how to get him into her bed, but she couldn't think about that right now, not when Xander was standing in front of her looking like all her best birthdays rolled into one.

Her heart raged in her chest as she realised this was her opportunity to ask for what she really wanted. To make love to him. Feel him move inside her. Breathe in the clean scent of his skin and slide against him, over and over again until they were breathless. Something she'd been aching for all night.

No, strike that, since the first moment she'd set eyes on him at his studio in London.

As she walked towards him he looked round at her and gave her a tentative smile as if he wasn't sure how he should act around her today. 'Good morning,' he said, his voice low and sweet.

Without saying a word, she put out a shaking hand and pressed it against the rock-hard muscles of his chest and felt his sharp intake of breath. Encouraged that he hadn't slapped her hand away, she took a step closer to him and forced herself to look up into his face.

He stared down at her with an open, questioning look in his eyes. Summoning all her courage, she pushed up on her tiptoes and leant in towards him, her lips tingling in readiness for the feel of his mouth against hers.

His breath was coming out in shortened gasps and she felt it whisper against her skin for a moment before their lips connected.

A low, almost animal sound came from deep within his chest as she slipped her tongue against the ridge of his teeth. Opening his mouth against her tentative invasion, he flexed his tongue against hers and she tasted the sweetness of him, her body reacting immediately to a desperate need to be enfolded in his arms and held close.

He let her take control as she slid her fingers into his hair and drew him even closer. Leaning into him, she felt the solid ridge of his body press against her from pelvis to chest.

He wanted her, she noted with a breathless sort of glee—she could feel it in the tension of his muscles and, more to the point, in the hard bulge at the front of his trousers.

With shaking hands, she fumbled with his belt, her clumsy fingers making slow work of unbuckling it.

She didn't allow herself to stop to think about what she was doing. She couldn't. If she let anything other than her determination to feel him inside her flit through her head she'd stall and the moment would be lost for ever. And that meant never being able to have what she so badly wanted.

To indulge her fantasies for once in her life.

To let go of her anxiety and just take what she wanted.

And she wanted this. So much it hurt.

She was *going* to take it and decorum be damned.

The buckle finally came apart and she popped the button on the front of his trousers and slid her hand inside them, under his underwear, until she found the hardness of him. She drew away and looked up into his face.

His eyes were hazy with a need she felt sure must be reflected in her own.

'Don't stop,' he growled, his voice so low she could barely make out the words.

Wrapping her hand around the length of him, she moved her fingers from base to tip, catching the velvety soft head with her thumb and feeling the slickness of his arousal coat her fingertips.

'Ah, hell, Jess, that feels so good.' His fingers wound into her hair, pulling her mouth towards him and kissing her so thoroughly she thought she might die from the pleasure of it.

His hands skimmed beneath the hem of her dress and slid up her thighs, his fingers tugging at the elastic of her knickers so hard she felt it ping and give as the seam ripped and the scrap of material fell to the floor.

'Oops, sorry,' Xander said against her mouth, not sounding in the least bit sincere.

She giggled as he kissed across her cheek and gently tickled the sensitive whorl of her ear with his tongue, but soon stopped as she felt his fingers find the slick heat between her legs.

Pressing against his hand, she felt the beginnings of an orgasm stir deep in her pelvis and the need to have the hard length of him inside her grew even more intense. She'd been picturing this situation in her head all night and now that the possibility it might actually happen had arisen she could barely wait. She felt greedy for it.

'Xander...'

'Yeah,' he groaned, as if sensing she was about to cut their encounter short and readying himself to be a gentleman about it.

'Do you still want me hard and fast against the wall?' she asked, forcing herself to look him directly in the eye. If this was the last chance she was going to get to test out just how brazen she could push herself to be, she wanted to go all the way.

'Hell, yeah,' he breathed in relief, reaching a hand round to grab his wallet out of the back pocket of his trousers. Releasing his hold on her, he located a condom before dropping the wallet onto the floor next to them.

He didn't move his gaze away from hers as he waited for her to step back so he could strip off his clothes.

She'd never seen anyone get undressed so fast.

He stood there naked in front of her, the heat of his body radiating outwards, warming her skin with its fiery intensity. Taking a deep breath, she allowed her gaze to travel down the magnificence of him, taking in every beautiful dip and curve.

Her gaze returned to his and locked for a moment as he checked with her silently that she really wanted this.

'Yes,' she said, and he gave her a smile of such un-adulterated pleasure she nearly came on the spot.

He took a moment to sort out the condom, before returning his gaze to hers, his eyebrow raised in a se-ductive challenge.

'You ready for me, Jess?'

'As I'll ever be,' she replied, suddenly horrendously shy about what was about to happen. But before she had time to dwell on it, he stepped forward, and, putting a hand on each of her upper arms, walked her backwards until her shoulders slammed against the wall. His mouth came down on hers immediately and she was lost in an electric storm of need, her body throbbing with want, want, *want*.

His body enveloped hers, pressing into her with a power she'd never experienced before. She *knew* she was wanted because she could *feel* it in him.

His hands raked up under her skirt again, bunching it up around her waist, exposing her to his exploring fin-gers. He moved them against her, then inside her until she thought she'd go crazy with it, bringing his mouth hard down onto hers at the same time, the dual stimu-lation sending her senses into overdrive.

She was so on the edge it wasn't funny.

'Now, Xander, I want…' she gasped.

He waited a moment for her to continue, then stilled his movement until she looked back into his eyes. 'Tell me what you want, Jess.'

'I want you. Inside me.' The words left her lips as though they'd been primed and were just waiting for the opportunity to finally be said. It was easy, so easy now she'd given herself permission not to care about anything other than what was happening between them at that moment.

He didn't need anything more from her. Sliding a hand down the inside of her thigh, he hooked his wrist under her leg and drew it up against his waist. The rigid tip of his erection penetrated the slick opening to her a second later, and she gasped with pleasure as he slowly slid inside her.

They began to move together, Xander pressing her hard into the wall to support them both as he thrust, filling her completely and hitting a sweet spot over and over as their bodies crashed together. They kissed hard, their mouths swollen and hungry as their tongues delved, tasting each other. Grasping the buttoned-down front of her dress, Xander pulled it apart hard, ripping the delicate buttons away from the material so they pinged and bounced across the room. The material gaped at the front, exposing her breasts, encased in the lacy bra she'd chosen to wear on a whim that morning and she didn't even think to react as he pushed aside the cups to expose the hard peaks of her nipples to his searching fingers.

Jess thought she might go crazy from the pulsing heat between her legs and the gentle rasp of Xander's touch on her exposed nipples. But she wasn't there yet; it wasn't quite enough.

'Xander…I need… I need…'

Seeming to sense her frustration, he dipped his hand between their bodies, sliding the pad of his fingertip against her clitoris, mimicking the movement of his thrusts inside her.

Gripping the bulk of his shoulders for support, Jess

closed her eyes and allowed the delicious friction to build and intensify, sending waves of exquisite pleasure radiating out from deep within the centre of her, teetering on the edge of an orgasm for utterly crazed moments, before finally breaking into a rush of the most intense pleasure she'd ever experienced. A low guttural moan grew from the base of her throat and vibrated in the air around them as she totally lost control.

It only took Xander a couple more thrusts before he joined her in her electric ecstasy, pounding into her hard as he came, his breath hot and fast on her neck as he surged into her.

They remained like that for a while, both gasping for breath as they came back down to earth.

Finally able to relax her fingers enough to release her grip on his shoulders, Jess put her palms against his chest and pushed gently until he dipped and slid out of her. He took a step away so she could put both feet back on the ground.

They stood and looked at each other for a beat, their breathing still low and rough from their exertions, before they pulled themselves together.

Xander disposed of the condom while she readjusted her clothes, trying in vain to reclose the top of her dress where it now gaped open after his callous treatment of it.

'You owe me a dress,' she said, raising a mock-stern eyebrow.

He laughed. 'I think it looks better like that.' He ran a hand over her hair, smoothing it against her head. 'Let's lie down before we fall down,' he said, cocking a suggestive eyebrow. Taking her hand, he led her out of the studio and into his room.

He flopped down onto the bed, pulling her down

next to him, his naked body gleaming in the soft, late-morning light.

She couldn't tear her eyes away from the magnificent strength of him as he lay stretched out next to her. Her gaze raked him from head to toe, only snagging momentarily on the deep V where his hips joined his body, and lower...

He raised a questioning eyebrow as their gazes met again and she tried in vain to quell the rush of heat that travelled up her neck to burn her cheeks.

'Like what you see, Jess?'

'Absolutely,' she said, brazening it out. 'I can barely believe I've just "made it" with the third sexiest man in England,' she said, giving him a wide grin.

'Now do you believe the hype?' Xander joked, one discerning eyebrow raised. He nodded down to where the source of her most recent pleasure lay nestled against his thigh.

'Well, I guess there is some truth to those rumours.'

'You're very kind.' He chuckled, giving her such a sexy, playful look she wanted to lock him up and keep him all for herself for ever.

They lay together, limbs wrapped around each other, drowsy and sated in the growing heat of the morning.

Xander shifted onto his side, propping himself up onto one elbow. 'Why don't you stay on a while longer? It seems a shame to cut things short now when there's so much fun still to be had.' He raised a provocative eyebrow. 'I'm going to need *something* fun to do after a gruelling day of being all artistic.'

'*Something* fun to do?'

'Okay, some*one* fun to do.' He grinned.

Her heart hammered hard against her chest as she realised he was actually serious. 'I don't know, Xander—won't you need to concentrate on your exhibition?'

'Not in the evenings.'

Where had this sudden panicky feeling come from? She'd been all right brazening this out when she'd thought it would be a one-off and she'd be back home the following day, before she had chance to get too attached.

'I don't think I can. Pamela, the editor at the magazine I work for, is expecting me back at work tomorrow.'

'Can't you tell them you're ill or something? I'm sure she can cope without you for one more week.'

There was a weird rushing in her head that was making it hard for her to concentrate. 'I can't do that. What if she finds out I'm lying? I'll lose my job.'

'How would she find out if you're stuck in Italy, unable to travel? It's not as if she's going to jump on a plane with a cold compress and a bowl of chicken soup.'

Her heart was beating so fast she felt sure he must be able to see it pulsing against her chest. 'I don't feel comfortable with lying, Xander.'

'Don't you think you deserve some fun? Why are you so hard on yourself? It's like you don't believe you deserve to be happy or something.'

She sighed, rubbing a hand over her face.

He was right. She was a mess.

'I don't know why—I've always been like that. I have a highly developed guilty conscience and I get over-anxious about things sometimes. My mum always made me feel like it'd be the end of the world if I did anything to show her up and I guess it's just stuck around in my psyche. She expected perfection and I failed to deliver.'

He gave her a puzzled frown.

'I know, it's weird. Not something most people can understand.'

'Well, I think it's about time you came and joined me on the dark side.'

She laughed and shook her head. 'Why are you so intent on corrupting me?'

'Because it's fun to see you coming to pieces.' He ran a finger from the deep hollow in the base of her neck, down between her partly exposed breasts to where her belly button lay hidden beneath the cotton of her dress. 'Especially when I'm the one that gets to make you come.'

She put her hand over his, stopping him from continuing his path.

He closed his eyes and took a breath. 'Look, I'm not going to pressure you into this. If you don't want to stay, that's fine, but you should consider doing something wild and totally selfish, just for once.' He rolled away from her and got up, pulling on a pair of trousers. God, he looked sexy, half dressed like that with his hair all mussed and falling over his eyes.

Dishevelled and dangerous.

She suddenly wanted to stay. So much.

'I have to go and speak to my agent about the arrangements for the exhibition. Come and find me if you change your mind.'

He gave her one last heated look before turning and leaving the room, pulling the door closed behind him.

The ensuing silence of the room filled her head until she thought she'd go crazy with it.

The thought of never seeing him again left her feeling empty. Totally and utterly empty. He was right: she should allow herself to do something completely crazy for once. She was sick and tired of worrying about doing the right thing all the time. After all, Pamela said she needed to *live a little* if she was going to become a better writer.

Returning to her bedroom, she retrieved her mobile phone from the nightstand, readying herself to put on her most ill-sounding voice, and called through to the magazine.

'Pamela Bradley.'

Just the sound of her editor's voice made her stomach twitch with nerves.

'Hi, Pamela, it's Jess.'

'Jess, are you on your way back?'

She took a deep, steadying breath. 'Er, actually, I think I've picked up that flu that was going around the office before I left for Italy.' She gave a fake cough, willing Pam to believe her. She was so nervous about lying her palms were sweaty and her body felt hot and tingly. She'd never played hooky in her life and it made her really uncomfortable to lie like this, but the draw of spending a little more time with Xander fortified her.

'I can work on the story from my bed,' she rushed on into Pam's silence, feeling her cheeks flame as guilt swept through her. 'I only need a few more days to get it nailed down, then I'll email it over. You're going to love it, Pam. He's such an interesting subject to write about,' she said, inordinately relieved Pamela couldn't see how red her face was.

Liar, liar, pants on fire couldn't have been more appropriate at that moment.

There was a long pause, then a sigh. 'Okay, Jess, but make sure you hit your deadline. I need this piece in on time otherwise you're going to find yourself right at the top of the redundancy recommendation list.'

Jess swallowed hard. 'Okay, Pamela, I'll get it to you on time, I promise.'

She cut the call and put her phone carefully back onto the nightstand, feeling something she hadn't felt since childhood.

Naughty.

She'd never even contemplated playing hooky before she met Xander—never lied to get what she wanted. Even the thought of doing something so against the rules she lived by would have given her the heebie-jeebies before she met him, but now she'd crossed the line she was amazed by how enlightened she felt. How alive. As if her sluggish blood had woken up and decided to have a drag race around her body.

She guessed it was something to do with endorphins, this crazy recklessness, some mad chemical reaction. It was certainly like a drug, this throbbing, screaming urge to break out of her normal, dull existence and do something crazy for once.

Her usual control seemed to have abandoned her, at least for a short while, and she felt buzzed and high on life, as if there was a world of possibility out there for her—something that had hidden from her consciousness up until this point, something that had only ever happened to other people.

Xander had unearthed a part of herself she never knew was there. She wasn't sensible, dependable, unremarkable Jess when she was with him; she was exciting, stimulating, *wild*.

She was out of breath when she returned to Xander's studio. He opened the door with an expectant smile.

'I don't have anything planned for the next week,' she gasped. 'So I'm all yours.'

He grinned. 'All mine. I like the sound of that.'

CHAPTER EIGHT

THEY SPENT THE first couple of days in and out of bed together, taking time out for a couple of hours here and there so that Xander could squirrel away in his studio to work on the exhibition and Jess could explore more of Lake Garda, gathering information for her holiday piece.

Each time they made love, Jess would allow him to reveal a little more of her body until she was almost comfortable with him seeing her naked.

It was a revelation.

The whole thing was also a huge step away from reality—something Jess had to keep forcibly reminding herself about.

Every now and again a little bubble of hope that they could turn this fling into something more rose in her chest and she'd have to stamp on it hard to stop herself from getting carried away with the idea.

She needed to keep this thing in perspective. It *wasn't* real and she was going to have to wake up soon and rejoin the real world. This was a holiday from life, pure and simple.

Attaching any kind of emotion to it would be an utter disaster.

* * *

Partway into the week, Jess woke to find Xander had got up before her for once. After getting dressed and grabbing some breakfast, which Rosa served out on the veranda, she went looking for him.

The sun was already beating down and she wanted to go for a swim in the lake and hoped she might be able to persuade him to go with her.

He was in his studio, flinging paint from a brush onto a large canvas on the floor. More tarp-covered canvases were propped up against all four walls and his art table was laden with tubes of paint and sketch pads. She wondered what she would see if she peeked underneath the tarpaulins. He'd refused to let her look at what he was working on, saying he never let anyone see an unfinished painting, and she was slightly nervous about whether he'd used any of the sketches of her.

'Will you come for a swim? It's so hot today,' she said, moving closer to the art table and glancing down to see if she could see whether any of his sketch pads were open.

They weren't.

'Not right now. I'm in the middle of this. You go.'

He turned away again, and swiped at the canvas, already lost in his secret little world. The rejection stung. Was she really going to let him get away with ignoring her like that?

No. She certainly wasn't.

Picking up a paintbrush from the table, she dipped it in a discarded palette of rich, purple paint. It was gloopy enough to hang onto the brush for a second or two before dripping back down into the pool of shiny, slick liquid. Turning back to him, she raised the brush to ear level, then brought it forward quickly, flicking the paint towards him. It landed with a splatter against his golden skin, a line of dots making their unsubtle way from his shoulder blade to his hip.

He swivelled round and looked at her, startled. 'What the hell was that?' he said, raising a challenging eyebrow.

She grinned. 'I thought I'd paint you for a change. You look good in purple, but then you look good in everything.'

He huffed out a laugh before turning back to his easel.

Outraged at his snubbing, she moved round so she was standing facing him, just behind the easel. She flicked another splodge of paint, which caught him on his chest this time, right above his nipple.

His eyebrows shot up as he lifted his head slowly to look at her again. 'Are you sure you want to start a paint fight with me, Miss Prim? How will you ever cope with getting paint on your perfectly clean and pressed clothes?'

'You wouldn't dare,' she teased, delighted she'd been able to capture his attention.

'You're playing a dangerous game, Jess. Don't think I won't retaliate. I have a whole palette of colours here with your name on it. Just try it one more time.'

She gave him a slow, taunting smile, her blood pumping fast through her veins as an urge to see exactly what he had planned caught her by the throat.

Her hand quivered by her side.

She really should put the paintbrush down and go for a walk or something to relieve this crazy impulse to keep pushing him. It was madness, this whole thing.

He was watching her, his eyes narrowed with suspicion. Anticipating her next move.

Did she dare?

Yes, she did.

Turning back to the table, she loaded up the brush with paint again, then twisted back, holding it aloft.

'Je-e-ess.' Xander's voice was low with warning, but she caught the lilt of amusement.

The look in his eye made her insides flip, but some craziness compelled her to bring back her hand and let the paint fly through the air in his direction.

This time he dodged it and it sailed past him, splattering the floor behind where he stood.

With a dangerously predatory grin, he advanced towards her, loaded paintbrush held aloft.

Adrenaline-fuelled blood pumped through her as her fight-or-flight instinct kicked in. In her real life she'd be putting her hand up to stop this right now, to save her clothes as well as her pride, but this time she didn't want it to stop. She wanted to experience the heady rush of excitement as she let whatever might happen happen. She ached to feel his hands on her, his body pressed close to hers again, their skin slippery and messy with paint.

Where had this wild abandon come from? She hardly recognised herself.

He was almost upon her now, his bright aqua gaze trained on her face.

'No, no, Xander, wait,' she stuttered, feigning fright.

'What's the matter, Jess—can't stand to get down and dirty with me?'

She took the opportunity in his pause to tease her to sneak in another crafty flick of her brush, sending the paint higher this time so it landed squarely across his nose and cheeks.

He stared at her in utter disbelief for a nanosecond,

before letting out a low growl and flicking his own brush at her over and over again, covering her T-shirt, her jeans and her hair in bright magenta paint.

Tipping back his head, he laughed at the mock horror on her face. 'You look good in hot-pink, Jess. You should wear it more often.' He took a step towards her and her stomach did a slow roll with excitement. 'But I have to say, I think you'd look a lot better in just the paint.'

She held his gaze as he stared her down, the dare behind his words overt in his expression.

'Okay.' Before she lost her nerve, she pulled the ruined T-shirt up over her head and dropped it on the floor next to her.

Xander's brows shot up in surprise. 'What's this? Not going feral on me, are you?' he asked, his voice catching as she reached round and unhooked her bra with shaking fingers, letting it fall to the ground beside her. Closing her eyes, she willed her erratic breathing to normalise. She could swear she felt the heat of his gaze sweeping her upper body, taking in the fullness of her breasts and the hard jut of her nipples as she stood there in front of him.

Totally exposed.

Totally vulnerable.

Something cool and soft swept over her left breast and she gasped in shock at the alien sensation.

Snapping open her eyes, she saw that Xander was running the tip of his paintbrush over her skin, circling the bud of her nipple in slow, seductive strokes. She shivered with pleasure as he flicked it upwards, then began to make wider sweeping circles around her breasts.

Her skin felt so sensitive she trembled every time he moved his brush to a new area.

Without moving his gaze from her face, Xander backed away to where his easel stood propped up in the middle of the room. Reaching down, he grabbed his palette loaded with paint and walked back to where she stood.

By now she was shaking with nerves, but she made herself stand there, rooted to the spot, unflinching as he tested her nerve.

Without saying a word, he unpopped the buttons of her jeans with his spare hand and slid them down her legs until they pooled in a heap at her feet. Next, he slipped his cool fingers into the waistband of her knickers and slid those down, too, with slow, excruciating care, until she stood naked before him.

His gaze glided up and down her body and she shifted on her feet, but steadfastly kept her arms at her sides, allowing him to look.

'Beautiful,' he murmured, his voice low and deep.

He covered her body in paint, keeping his strokes long and slow until she thought she'd go crazy with it. She wanted to feel him, sliding against her skin, the paint lubricating their movement, so she reached for him, pulling his T-shirt over his head, and he helped her undress him, casting off the remainder of his clothes.

After slicking her hands over her paint-covered body, she pressed them against his chest, leaving a stark handprint over each pec, delighting in his sharp intake of breath as she then swiped her palms over and over his nipples. Looking up into his handsome face, she caught his eye and grinned, then swiped more paint across his stomach and down his arms, laughing at his comical expression, until he stopped her by pulling her close and kissing her hard, skin sliding against skin, making a sucking sound as they came apart and pressed back together.

Jess laughed in glee. 'You're going to have to come for a swim now to wash all this off.'

Xander raised an eyebrow. 'Later,' he said, his voice seductively low. 'Once we've explored just how dirty we can get.'

Xander woke early again the next day and got up to see the sun rising on the other side of the lake, spreading its soft rays across the water and tipping the buildings with a warm honey-coloured glow.

Looking back at the bed where Jess lay, the sheet barely covering her naked body, he felt a harmony he hadn't experienced in a very long time. She looked so peaceful, so content, so relaxed for once.

Moving quietly over to the bed so as not to wake her, he tugged gently on the sheet until it slipped off her, revealing her beautiful, voluptuous form in all its glory.

He could only just make out the profile of her face in the gentle glow of the morning light. Her arms and legs lay splayed towards each corner of the bed as if she'd been tied down, her spirit trapped in the amazing body she'd loathed so much. As he moved towards her his tired eyes played tricks on him in the low-level light and a double image of her appeared in his vision, as if that fighting spirit of hers had risen like a dark angel from where she lay trapped and was hovering above her body.

He had a moment of pure, clear inspiration as his imagination twisted the image so her spirit was floating above her fully clothed and trapped human form as she lay bound to the bed.

It was the final image he needed for the exhibition.

A picture of her naked spirit, stripped of all her in-hibitions. Beautiful and real and breaking free.

Hands shaking, he picked up his sketch pad and pen-cil, sat in the chair at the end of the bed and began to draw.

In that moment, he wanted things to stay like this for ever, but he knew, with a sinking feeling in his chest, that life wasn't like that—he wasn't like that—and when the time came for her to leave he would say goodbye without putting up a fight.

He really needed to pull himself together and focus his attention on finishing his pictures for the exhibi-tion now or he was never going to hit his deadline. He couldn't go on the way he was, unfocused and unprofes-sional, or it would be the end of his career as an artist. People would forget about him, and he really couldn't allow that to happen.

The thought of running out of money and having to work a real job again, like the soul-destroying ones he'd done to stay alive as a teenager, filled him with cold dread. He was terrified by the idea of not feeling special or revered any more—of being ordinary again.

He couldn't let this thing with Jess get in the way. Whatever had happened between them didn't feel like the usual artist-muse relationship, and it made him un-easy. This fling with her had rejuvenated him but he needed to step away from it now.

This was the beginning of the end.

On their last morning together, he sketched her as she sat on the terrace sipping a cup of coffee, looking out across the lake. She looked so beautiful—her amaz-ingly expressive face alive with the vitality that had first drawn her to him. She seemed like a different woman from the one he'd met only a couple of weeks ago. She was taller, brighter and somehow more real.

She'd found her joy.

When she turned and smiled back at him, her perfect white teeth flashed between her lips. Even her smile was more relaxed since he'd first met her.

Was that because of him?

He felt a swell of pride at the thought. He'd never made anyone *less* stressed before.

The intimacy of the atmosphere tugged at his chest. The thought that this was just a fleeting moment in his life made him clench his jaw, and a low throb began to beat in his temple. Why did that bother him so much? What was this feeling? He wasn't entirely sure. He'd never experienced it before, but he sure as hell didn't like it.

He'd been bored and frustrated when he'd asked Jess to come to Italy. It had been a spur-of-the-moment thing—just for kicks—but he'd underestimated her ability to get into his head. To find out what it was that drove him. To discover his deepest, darkest secrets. And he'd let her probe and push until all the bad memories that he'd buried for so long had begun to rise to the surface.

He didn't want to feel like this. After spending the majority of his life pushing that anxiety and fear of rejection away, he didn't want to have to face it now. He wanted things to stay the way they were: light and free and easy.

He realised she was staring at him in confusion now and he adjusted the scowl on his face into a smile.

The apprehensive expression in her eyes made him wonder what she was thinking, but he didn't want to ask. Didn't want to know. Ignorance was bliss.

In retrospect, it had been a crazy move to ask a journalist to come and stay, then invite her into his bed. Of course she was going to push and push at his defences until she found a crack to get her nails into.

It was her job.

He needed to remind himself of that.

She shifted in her chair, putting her coffee cup down onto the table with a shaky hand. 'I guess I should go and write my article. Pamela's going to kick my butt if I send it in late and I haven't even started it yet,' she said, awkwardly rising from her seat so that she banged her leg on the table.

Was she feeling the same tension that he was?

He shrugged off his concern and nodded at her stiffly. 'Okay. See you later.'

Jess sat in the middle of the bed with all her notes spread around her. She was hyperaware that this was the last day they had together, but she had to get this article written. This was why she'd come here, after all.

Xander had seemed to become increasingly distanced from her over the last couple of days, which had unsettled her, and she'd thought the best thing to do right now was to get away from the intensity of their situation for a while and try and get her head straight.

This piece on Xander had to be the very best thing she'd ever written or there was a very good chance she'd be booted off the magazine as soon as she got back.

As she scanned over and over all the notes she'd written since she'd arrived a stultifying fear started to grip her. What if she couldn't do it? The words began to blur together and the more she read, the more panicked she got.

After about half an hour of trying and failing to write

one single usable sentence, she gathered up every piece of paper, shuffled them into one tidy sheaf, then threw them across the room in frustration.

She watched as they floated down like overlarge snowflakes and settled onto the cold, tiled floor.

This was ridiculous. How the hell was she ever going to be able to write a thing? Closing her eyes, she took a moment to think back over the time she'd spent here with Xander, about his passion and fears, and his determination not to be beaten down by them and finally how he'd made her feel by including her in his life. How he'd brought out a side of her she'd never known was there.

A deep, bolstering warmth pulsed through her.

Pulling her laptop towards her, she let her fingers move over the keyboard, writing whatever came into her head without letting conscious thought intrude, without giving in to her fear about whether what she was writing was any good or not. Instead, she concentrated on how Xander made her feel about herself.

And the words began to flow. It was as if she'd finally keyed into something—opened a previously locked door in her brain; now all these intense thoughts and feelings, which she'd been suppressing for so long, began firing round her brain.

She wrote and wrote and edited and wrote some more until there it was—the best thing she'd ever written. Reading it back, she had tears in her eyes. It had warmth and humour and, best of all, fire and life. She knew in her gut that Pamela was going to love it—that it might just save her career.

She also knew without a doubt that she was totally and utterly in love with Xander.

And that she'd failed to follow the most basic rule

of all: don't fall for a guy who's incapable of loving you back.

Somewhere in the back of her brain she'd harboured the hope that the time they'd spent together had meant more to him than any of his previous nonrelationships, and that this time he wanted more.

That he wanted her as she wanted him.

But she knew she was kidding herself—just look at how detached he'd been with her this morning. This relationship was only ever a temporary thing for him. For both of them. A whimsy, a folly, a lark.

What had he called it?

A blip in their timeline.

He'd made that very clear.

She had to pull herself together.

Not giving herself time to fuss and start fiddling with a word here and a word there, she attached the document she'd just written to an email to Pam and hit send, and it was gone—her future—off into the ether.

Her time here was finished.

All she had to do now was say goodbye.

Feeling as if her feet were made of lead, she searched the house for Xander, finding him painting madly away in his studio, in what seemed to have become his usual zoned-out state over the last couple of days. She watched him for a few minutes, taking in the graceful fluidity of his movements as he swiped his brush across the canvas. He was frowning hard in concentration, his handsome face shuttered and drawn as he poured his soul onto the canvas.

He barely glanced up as she moved into the room.

She understood his utter absorption in what he was doing—she'd felt the same about her writing—and it was amazing to see him in such a frenzy of excited activity after being so agitated about not being able to make the magic happen before now. She liked to think she had something to do with that, in some small way.

Finally, he glanced up from what he was doing and noticed her standing there.

'Hey, Jess, how long have you been there?'

'Only a couple of minutes,' she said quietly.

He nodded distractedly. 'The exhibition's taking shape. It's all coming together.' The look in his eye was almost manic.

'Well, I'm really pleased for you,' she managed to force past the lump in her throat.

'Jess?' He was looking at her as if he was worried she was about to cry—which was pretty much on the money.

Pull yourself together, woman.

She didn't want him to see how upset she was about the inevitable end of their time together.

Glancing away, she smoothed her hair down against her head and fought against the growing tension in the back of her throat. She couldn't look at him any more. If she did he'd see just how much she was struggling to keep it together.

'I finished my article,' she said, attempting to keep the misery out of her voice.

'Oh, yeah?' He looked at her, his eyes blank, his mind obviously still on his painting.

'Don't worry, I gave you a good write-up and I didn't include anything too salacious.'

He smiled. 'Great, that's great, Jess. Congratulations.'

He looked back at his painting as if he'd said all there was to say.

She was being dismissed.

So this was it, then. The end of the affair.

'Okay, then, I guess I'd better let you get on with finishing your picture. Will you let me know when you're exhibiting? I'll leave my contact details on the hall table. I'd love to finally get to see what you've been working so hard on.'

He looked up at her again, the hazy look in his eyes clearing as if her words had finally penetrated through to his brain.

'Hell, Jess, sorry, I was right in the middle of a thought here. Yes, of course I'll let you know.'

There was a steely look in his eye now, as if he'd hardened himself against her.

A hot wave of despair crashed over her.

She needed to get out of there before she made a fool of herself and did something stupid and crass like asking him to be her *boyfriend*.

'Okay, then. Well, it's been a blast. Good luck.' Without waiting for a response, she turned on her heel and walked away from him, before he could see how much she wanted him to ask her not to go.

All the way through packing her suitcase she wondered whether he'd come and stop her.

As she walked down the corridor, then out of the villa, then got into her car, with her heart hammering against her chest, she wondered whether he'd come running up at the last moment and say, 'I want you to stay.'

Then as she drove the car slowly out of the driveway and crept down the lane to the main road, her breath short and a hard pressure behind her eyes, just waiting to spill over into tears, she wondered whether she'd see him in her rear-view mirror, running after her car.

But she didn't.

He wasn't coming. He was letting her go.

CHAPTER NINE

XANDER SPENT THE next couple of days trying to convince himself it was a good thing that Jess had gone. He needed to concentrate on getting the paintings finished and having her around would have been disruptive.

But he couldn't convince himself.

The loneliness bit at him, sinking its teeth deep and leaving him on edge and distracted.

After a couple more days of failing to summon the energy to finish the final painting he decided that Italy and seclusion weren't working for him any more. He needed sparkiness and life again and that meant going back to London.

As soon as he arrived back he went straight out to a party some friends were holding at a bar in Sloane Square, expecting the buzz of the city to perk him back up, but it didn't work.

He felt tired and drained and ended up going home unfashionably early, telling his friends it was because he'd expended so much energy on his art recently, but even as the words left his mouth he knew that wasn't the real reason. Normally when he was excited about a piece of art he was working on he was full of adrenaline—wanting to talk about it with everyone he met—but he felt protective about this exhibition for some reason.

He couldn't quite put his finger on why.

Jess had returned to London in a state of bewildered confusion.

Walking back into the buzz of the *Spark* office had been a shock to the system after the peace and tranquillity of Lake Garda and it took her a few days to get back up to speed with the London pace of life.

To her annoyance she'd found Pamela was off sick with the flu when she first arrived back and so hadn't even looked at the piece she'd written yet—perhaps it was karma catching up with her for playing hooky. The thought that she could have stayed for a couple more days with Xander flittered through her mind, but she knew that would have only prolonged the anxiety of having to say goodbye.

Despite her determination to get over Xander and move on with her life, she was having an awfully hard time getting him out of her head.

Spending time with him had been life-changing— letting loose without the fear of being judged had excited her more than she'd ever felt possible and she'd loved being touched and explored and worshipped, and having his delighted permission to do the same back to him. He'd woken something inside her that had been slumbering for years.

For the first time in her life she'd felt desired, sexy. Beautiful.

She found she was walking around now with her head held higher, making herself look at the world around her instead of staring down at the floor as she had before she'd met him. He'd opened up a whole world of possibility in her mind. Sex *was* something she could enjoy, and while it wasn't the be-all and end-all, it added an edge of excitement to her life that had previously been missing. Now she'd experienced great sex, she could barely believe she'd gone without it for so long.

The world seemed full of new possibilities, alive with promise.

But on the flip side, no Xander making her heart race and her blood pump with excitement just by being close.

She realised, of course, that she'd run away from him again, only this time he hadn't chased her. Perhaps he'd thought there was no point, that she didn't want him to ask her to stay? He wasn't a mind reader, after all, so how could he have known what she wanted?

She should have told him how she felt.

If she'd learnt anything over the last couple of weeks it was that she needed to put herself out there, to open herself up to new experiences if she wanted the opportunity for something good to happen. She couldn't just sit back any more, with her head in the sand, and wait for things to happen *to* her.

Pamela finally came back after a couple more days off sick and Jess waited, nerves jumping, to be summoned into her office.

'Well, Jess, I've read your piece on Xander Heaton,' Pamela said as Jess perched carefully on the edge of the seat facing the editor's desk. Jess managed a smile despite her jaw being clenched with anxiety.

She just wanted it to be over with so she could move forward. If Pamela still thought she couldn't cut it at *Spark* and she had to go back home and start again she wanted time to come to terms with the toe-curling horror of it.

'Well, you did it, you impressed me,' Pam said, and

Jess felt a lightness in her chest battle with the heaviness that had been keeping her company since she'd left Italy. 'This is exactly the kind of writing I'd been hoping to see. I don't know what happened out there, but whatever it was it's had a big effect on your style. I like it, Jess, well done.'

It was a big deal to her to hear that kind of praise from someone as tough as Pamela, and her eyes welled with grateful tears.

'So I get to keep my job here?' she asked breathlessly.

'Absolutely,' Pam replied.

Jess breathed a huge sigh of relief. At least that part of her life was on the right track again.

'The only thing it needs before it can go in the magazine is a mention of what he's working on at the minute,' Pamela said as Jess began to stand up, thinking she was home and dry.

She went hot, then cold in the space of a second. 'I—I don't know what he was working on,' she stammered. 'At least, he never let me see the pictures. He was really insistent about that.'

The look of displeasure on Pamela's face made her stomach sink.

'Well, you'll just have to go and see him and tell him you have a couple of follow-up questions. See if you can get a gander at the pictures while you're there,' her boss said flippantly, as if that would be the easiest thing in the world. 'From the tone of the article it sounded like you got to know him pretty well.' She raised a discerning eyebrow. 'Use your influence, Jess.'

Her chest felt tight and her lungs seemed to be having trouble drawing air. 'You want me to go all the way back to Italy to find out what he's working on?'

Pam gave her a withering look. 'Don't you read the

gossip columns? He's back in London. Although they're all chatting about the fact he left a party early for once instead of indulging in his usual bad behaviour.'

'Xander's b-back in London?' Jess managed to stutter through frozen lips.

When she'd thought he was still in Italy it had been easier to keep her heartache under wraps, but it felt as if he were close enough to touch now—close, yet still so far away.

Pam sighed and looked at her as if she thought she was talking to a total idiot. 'Yes, Jess. So get your hide over there and source what we need so I can put this issue to bed.'

Sliding off her chair and standing up on jellylike legs, Jess gave her editor a stiff nod. 'Okay, Pam, I'll see what I can do.'

Jess stood outside the door to Xander's studio, her body quivering with nerves and her heart in her mouth.

She had no idea how she was going to play this. She also didn't know how he was going to react when he saw her again. They hadn't exactly parted on bad terms, but there hadn't been a fond farewell either.

Perhaps this was fate or serendipity, or whatever you wanted to call it, handing her an opportunity. Perhaps when he saw her he'd realise how they were meant to be together and ask her not to leave again.

Perhaps.

Only one way to find out.

Before she lost her nerve, she lifted her shaking hand and banged hard on his door, hoping he was in there.

After a couple of seconds the door flew open to reveal Xander in all his splendour, regulation paintbrush in hand and a look of acute surprise on his face when he clocked that it was her on his doorstep.

'Jess!' His beautiful voice rumbled through her, waking up every nerve ending and sending a rush of pure longing south through her body. He was even more gorgeous, more virile, than she remembered. It had been less than a week since they'd last seen each other, but to Jess it felt like a lifetime since she'd been allowed to touch him.

She wanted him back. So badly it physically hurt.

She needed to be cool here, collected and poised. No way was she going to go to pieces and make a fool of herself.

Opening her mouth to speak, she froze, totally at a loss for what to say now she was standing there in front of him again.

Say something, Jess. Anything.

'I love you,' she blurted, her brain too late to catch up with her mouth and circumnavigate the damage she'd just wreaked.

He just stared at her with those mesmerising eyes of his and didn't say a word. There wasn't even a flicker of emotion on his face.

Her heartbeat accelerated as she waited for something—anything—to give her a clue about how he felt about her laying herself on the line like that.

There was a sound of heavy footsteps behind her and, grateful for the distraction from her humiliation, she broke her awkward eye contact with Xander and turned around to see a thickset, silver-haired man reach the top of the stairwell and raise a hand in greeting to them both.

'Xander, glad I've caught you in. I've been speaking to the guys at the Brick Lane gallery and they have a couple more questions about how we want to set the exhibition up. I was in the area so I thought I'd drop in for a quick chat about it.'

Jess heard Xander clear his throat behind her. 'Sure, Paul, yeah. Tell you what, come down to the kitchen with me while I make a drink for my guest and we'll chat on the way.'

Jess's skin prickled as she felt him move from behind her and she watched in stultified silence as he walked towards his visitor.

He turned back to look at her, his face still devoid of any emotion.

'Jess, why don't you wait in my studio? I'll be back in a minute and we can talk,' he said levelly.

She gave him a nod and a tentative smile, then watched him disappear down the stairs after his visitor.

Stumbling into his studio, she closed the door behind her and put her head in her hands. She stared at the floor in horror, utterly incredulous that she just *told him that she loved him.*

Well, at least no one could accuse her of beating around the bush.

What must he be thinking right now? And what was he going to say when he finally came back into the room?

Her heart thumped against her chest as she considered the possibilities. Rejection or acceptance. Whichever he chose, it was going to turn her world upside down. Again.

She paced the room for a minute trying to get her head together, managing to knock into one of the paintings propped against the wall and jumping back when it fell flat against the floor with a clatter.

Picking it up, she propped it back against the wall

and knelt there for a moment, breathing slowly and deeply. As she stared at the back of the painting it suddenly occurred to her that she was alone, in Xander's studio, surrounded by his exhibition paintings. Well, she might as well get what she'd come here for while he was out of the room. Even if he gave her the brushoff she could still go back and give Pamela what she needed for the article before heading off home to crumple into a sobbing heap.

She walked unsteadily over to where his largest paintings stood, their paint-stained tarpaulins hiding them from sight. Her hand shook as she pulled up the bottom of one of the tarps to reveal the painting underneath.

Her heart rattled in her chest as she stood there, staring at it, hardly able to believe what she was seeing. It was a picture of her, standing naked, covered in paint with an embarrassingly provocative look on her face.

She could barely breathe, the horror of what she was seeing making her chest contract painfully.

Turning round, and with a sense of impending dread, she lifted up the tarp on the painting propped against the easel in the middle of the room. It was another one of her, lying trussed up to his bed, fully clothed in her linen suit and another image of her naked body above that in some subversive sexual pose.

He'd taken their most intimate, most intensely personal moments and was intending to use them for commercial gain.

The thought of these pictures being displayed in public view, her face clearly recognisable, made her want to vomit.

He didn't care about her at all; he'd been using her.

* * *

Xander somehow managed to deal with his agent's jovial banter and answer his questions about details for the exhibition while Jess's declaration that she *loved him* whirled like a tornado around his head.

He'd been amazed and strangely uplifted to find her standing there at his door, and seeing her again had brought home to him just how much he'd missed her company. But her announcement had thrown him for six.

Even though she'd clearly let it slip by accident—in her usual impulsive fashion—he could tell from the look in her eye that she meant it.

And it scared the crap out of him.

For the first time in his life he had no idea how to deal with a situation. Usually he'd just blow a woman off if she suddenly announced she was in love with him, but he didn't want to do that with Jess. She meant more to him than that.

He just wasn't sure how much more.

They needed to talk about this, that was for damn sure.

After finally getting rid of Paul, he walked back into the studio to find Jess standing in front of the final painting he'd been working on for the exhibition—the one of her sexual epiphany. His first instinct was to stride over there and pull the tarp back down and yell at her for peeking, until he saw the look of bewildered disbelief on her face.

'You sketched me naked? While I was asleep?' She sounded so shocked, so hurt, it stopped him in his tracks. He approached her with his hands held out in a placatory gesture, as a dark, disturbing burn wove through his chest and pooled in his belly. 'Jess, it was amazing. I had this moment of clarity—I haven't been this excited about a painting in a very long time.'

She stared at him, aghast. 'You thought it would be okay, when you knew how much I hated showing my body? I haven't exactly been coy about that, Xander, but you thought you'd go ahead and do it anyway without me knowing about it?'

A cold shiver tickled down his spine. 'I thought maybe you'd got past the worry about how you look naked.'

'You thought you'd fixed me?' she interrupted. 'That after you'd thrown a few orgasms my way I'd suddenly love my body enough to have you expose it for *all the world to see*?' Her voice was shaking now. 'It was meant to be just for you, Xander. I never would have let you seduce me if I thought you were going to do something like this. You exploited my trust.'

'Jess, you're overreacting…'

'Do you have any idea how humiliated I feel right now? I trusted you. I thought you were a good guy—a messed-up egomaniac, but a good guy at heart. But this was only ever about the art, wasn't it, Xander? For your own benefit. For your *career*.'

He was floundering now, at a loss how to explain himself. 'But you look so amazing.'

'That's not the point, Xander,' she said, giving him such a cold look he had to take a breath to steady himself.

Frustration twisted his guts. 'You want me to pull the picture from the exhibition? It's the best thing I've done in years, Jess. You inspired it. You should be proud.'

'Proud!' She spat the word out. 'Proud for everyone to know I was just another of your saps that you slept with to get what you wanted, then tossed aside? Judging by the fact you thought it was okay to produce pictures like this of me—' she jabbed her finger towards the canvas '—I don't think there's any chance you could love me back in the way I need you to. I thought perhaps you understood me, that our time together meant something, but apparently I was wrong. I was naive and stupid to think I could be the woman to tame you. This was never about me, Xander, was it? It was always about you and your *art*.'

He couldn't answer. He couldn't even get his response to that straight in his head. He hadn't been looking for a relationship and this thing with Jess had just come out of the blue and now his creativity seemed to be peaking he was afraid to let anything get in the way of it. Thinking about someone else right now would take precious mental energy away from his work and he couldn't afford to let anything damage his muse again. Not even Jess.

He needed to prove to the world he was back, bigger, badder and stronger than ever. He'd won against the disabling inertia that had held him hostage for so long. He could prove his earlier talent hadn't been a fluke and stick two fingers up at all those naysayers.

To not let his father have been right about him.

Jess stared at him angrily for a beat longer, waiting in vain for him to pull himself together enough to answer her. When he failed to open his mouth, she turned on her heel and stormed out, slamming the door of the studio hard behind her.

He slumped into a chair, unable to process all the thoughts raging through his brain. He wanted her to be pleased and proud of his pictures, to tell him what good work he'd done, but instead she'd been more concerned about how she looked in them.

A disabling indolence kept him in his chair and he sat, staring into space as the silence echoed in his head.

Over the next few days he began to hate looking at his last painting of her, the initial joy of creating it marred by the pain and distress he'd caused.

After a couple more days of staring into space, he tried calling her, first on her mobile, only to be sent straight to voicemail, then at her magazine, only to be told she wasn't available and could they take a message?

He left numerous messages asking her to call him, becoming more and more irate when his phone remained steadfastly silent.

She'd cut him away like the bloodsucking leech he was.

It wasn't the first time a woman had walked out on him, but he'd never liked any of the others enough to care that much before. He liked Jess, though, an awful lot.

She'd twisted herself into his thoughts and he found himself on edge and preoccupied by the hole she'd left by her desertion. He barely knew her, but she'd done something to his psyche by forcing him to think about someone other than himself for once—as if she'd opened up a gaping chasm in his consciousness, which he was having trouble knitting back together.

He should have been honest with her about how he really felt, instead of treating her like some*thing* fun to do. He cringed at the memory of telling her that.

But he'd been scared. It was his standard defence mechanism, to keep his lovers at an emotional distance so he'd never have to deal with more of the painful feeling of rejection he'd been living with since he could remember.

His whole life had revolved around getting people

to buy into the image of the bad-boy loner he wanted them to see rather than the *real* him and he seemed unable to drag himself out of its deathlike grip.

Without meaning to he'd let Jess glimpse the real him, but when she'd pushed for more he'd thrown up his barriers, keeping their relationship purely physical, keeping her out.

Using her for his own ends.

He'd unequivocally demonstrated that his career was the most important thing in the world to him and that she'd meant nothing. He'd used her to fix himself, drained their relationship of everything good, then spat her out. Because he was a selfish idiot. His father had been right, after all; he didn't deserve to be loved, not when he acted the way he did. He took everything he wanted and gave nothing back.

He was pure, unadulterated greed.

If he was ever going to be good enough to be the right man for Jess he needed to learn how to let go of his anger and jealousy and fear and give her back what she'd given to him.

Humility and kindness and altruism. To learn how to give for the sake of giving, instead of looking for what he could get out of it.

He'd drawn himself into such a hard shell nothing had been able to penetrate it. Until Jess had come along and started tapping at the seams.

She'd been absolutely right about how distanced he'd allowed himself to be from everyone else, how hyper-focused he was about how things affected *him*. He'd completely overlooked how he'd messed up everyone else who came into contact with him, just so he could get what he wanted.

He'd been alone for so long he had no idea how to

let someone else into his life. How to care about them and let them care for him. Deep down he accepted now that he'd thought of himself as unlovable, after having it rammed home over the years through his dad's total lack of interest in him. He'd never admitted to his father how that had made him feel, he'd just shrugged it off as how things were, but he should have been braver. He should have stood up for himself instead of shutting himself away.

And now Jess had given up on him, too.

He wanted her back so much it made him ache, but how could he ever make her believe he meant it?

It was time to face up to what kept him so distanced from everyone else in his life.

He needed to let go of this feeling that he still had something to prove to a father who had never cared about him. The old man was dead and he needed to move on with his life now.

Then he needed to find Jess and convince her that he was sorry and that he was worth taking a risk on.

After days of not being able to face going in to his studio and hiding away from the world in his flat, he finally made the journey back there. Picking up a scalpel from in amongst the mess of paints and modelling equipment on his art table, he walked over to the painting of Jess. It was the piece of work that could prove he wasn't the flash in the pan that he, and pretty much everyone else in the world, it seemed, had feared he was.

Raising the scalpel, he brought it down hard across the canvas, cutting a large gash from corner to corner, then another, and another, until all that was left was a frame with colourful strips hanging from it like ragged paper garlands.

It was time to start again.

CHAPTER TEN

AFTER A FEW of weeks of going through the motions of getting up and going to work in a stultified daze, Jess finally began to come out of the emotional coma she'd put herself in in an attempt to block the pain and humiliation of how Xander had used her.

He'd tried calling her a couple of days after she'd first stormed out, which she'd ignored in her anger at him, but she hadn't heard from him since. He'd obviously given up on her now and she didn't expect ever to hear from him again. But then, why the hell would *she* be any different from the tens of women he'd already used up and cast aside? He'd probably moved on to a new love affair already.

She wouldn't know. She hardly looked at social media any more for fear of seeing something about him and a new lover that would bring back the flood of heartache she was only just starting to break through.

It was for the best. They would never have worked as a couple anyway. He was too self-involved, too wild, too ephemeral in nature for her and she couldn't match that.

Pulling off her coat and slumping into her chair at her desk, she was just about to turn on her computer when she noticed an envelope next to her keyboard, addressed to her at the magazine. The handwriting was loopy and messy and something about it made her heart beat a little faster. Tearing it open, she took out a piece of shiny black card and stared at it for a moment. It appeared to be blank, but when she went to flip it over something caught her eye. She tipped it back slowly until the fluorescent overhead lights in the office shone up the words: *Out of the Shadows. A new exhibition by Xander Heaton.*

Her heartbeat accelerated, sending a rush of adrenalised blood to her head, making her feel for a moment as if she might pass out. Taking a few deep breaths, she waited until the pounding in her head had calmed down before looking at the invitation again.

There was an address for a gallery in Brick Lane and a date and time for the following week in neat print below it.

Xander's exhibition.

Her naked body about to be exposed to the whole world.

The invitation slipped out of her trembling fingers and fell onto the floor. Looking down, she saw there were words scrawled on the back of it in the same looping handwriting that was on the envelope. Leaning down to peer closer at them, she made out the words, 'Jess, please come. I need you to see something. Xander'.

She stared at it for a few moments, the rushing sound in her ears blocking out the noise of the office. Sitting up, she jumped in shock when she realised Pamela had appeared out of nowhere and was standing over her, waiting for an answer to a question she'd totally failed to hear. Looking up to see her boss's imperious expression, she had to quell the nervous impulse to leap up and dash off to the sanctuary of the loos. 'Sorry, Pamela, I missed that.'

Pam shook her head, clearly unimpressed by Jess's lack of focus. 'I said, did you get an invitation to Xander Heaton's exhibition, too? He sent one to me asking me to make sure you came along. You must have made quite an impression on him.' She raised a perfectly plucked eyebrow.

'Ah, yes, but I wasn't going to go. I have a thing that night.'

Pamela's other eyebrow shot up to join its counterpart. 'Cancel it. You should attend. We could do a great follow-up piece on him for the magazine. Your interview's been syndicated to a lot of influential sources already and you're in a position to exploit your relationship with him to get a good exclusive interview afterwards. Am I right?'

Jess sighed. There was no way Pamela would let her get away with missing the exhibition if she thought the magazine had something to gain from it.

Well, she was going to have to face the horror of being recognised as the model in his paintings some time. It might as well be sooner rather than later. At least it might be a friendly crowd at the exclusive first showing of his work. She could write the piece, then go and hide away under a rock until all the fuss had died down.

She gave her editor a tight smile. 'Sure, Pamela, I'll be there.'

'Good, good. Make sure you work all the angles, Jess,' Pam said, waving a hand in the air as she stalked off, unquestionably on her way to terrorise another poor member of her staff.

Xander couldn't ever remember being this nervous before a showing of his work, and for once the nerves weren't about what the critics might say about it. It was all down to what Jess would think.

Everything he'd done here was for her, after all.

After she'd refused to pick up or return his phone calls he'd realised it was going to take more than words to prove to her he was sorry and that he cared about her and wanted to make a go of a relationship—something he'd never been interested in before. Unfortunately, his reputation for being such a playboy didn't do him any favours in that regard and he'd clearly fed directly into her insecurity about taking a relationship with him seriously with his selfish disregard for her feelings.

He missed her so much.

He couldn't go on the way he was, isolated and casually using people before casting them off like pieces of rubbish.

She'd shown him how incredible it could feel to fall in love with someone and now he'd experienced it he was damned if he was going to let her just walk away.

Because he *was* in love with her, he realised. This aching hole in his chest he'd been living with for the last two months was exactly Jess-sized.

The front door to the gallery swung open, bringing him back to the present and letting in a draught of cool evening air. He looked round to see who it was.

Jess.

He'd sent an invitation to her editor as well in the hope it would force Jess to come, but had made the time on Jess's half an hour earlier.

He wanted her to see what he'd done for her first without being interrupted.

Apparently this exhibition opening had turned into a hot ticket after Jess's article on him for *Spark* magazine had been so well received. He'd been humbled by her descriptions of him and impressed by how she'd woven in his background with real sensitivity, making him sound like the kind of guy he'd always wanted to be—intelligent, passionate and talented.

She'd let the piece run, showing him in such a good light, despite how he'd treated her.

He knew he didn't deserve to even lick her shoes, but he wanted to become a man who *did* deserve her, and only she could help him with that.

If she could forgive him.

She stood in front of him now, head held high, looking so beautiful and bold he wanted to pull her against him and kiss her hard, to let her know just how much he wanted her back. How amazing she was. But he knew he couldn't do that—he needed to be more subtle, to prove to her this wasn't just about sex.

'Where is everyone? Did I read the invitation wrong? I thought it started at seven thirty,' Jess said, staring at him defiantly, her arms folded across her chest. He could see she was trying to brazen it out, but her awkward stance and the slight tremor in her voice gave her away.

Maybe there was hope? The thought made his blood buzz with adrenaline.

'You're on time. This is a private viewing, just for you, before all the other guests arrive. I wanted you to be the first to see it.'

'So I have time to run away and hide before they all arrive?' she asked, an eyebrow quirked, clearly trying to keep her voice controlled, but failing spectacularly to hit the right note of nonchalance and sliding right on through to utter terror.

He put a reassuring hand on her shoulder, feeling the heat of her skin burn through her thin cotton top. His mind flicked back to the memory of how the heat of her body felt against his and he almost lost his cool.

'I'm really hoping you won't want to run,' he said, begging with his eyes for her to give him another chance.

'You know, I don't know if I can bear to look at it again, Xander.' Taking a step backwards, she broke his hold on her and gave him a wobbly smile. 'But I wish you luck with the exhibition. I'm sure everyone's going to love it.' She turned to walk away, but before she could take a step he slid his fingers around her arm and twisted her back round to face him. No way was he going to let her walk away before he had chance to at least apologise.

He pulled her hard towards him, drawing her mouth so tantalisingly close he could feel the heat of her breath on his lips. 'Jess, please. Don't leave. I did all this for you. Not for my critics. I wanted you to know how much I miss you. How much I care about you. Please don't walk away now.'

He felt her falter and relax a little against him and he pressed on quickly before she could gather herself enough to leave.

'This is my apology to you. No one has ever given me that much of themselves before, Jess, and I can't be-lieve I took advantage of you like that. I was so scared I was actually as washed up as everyone suspected, I lost sight of what was right and wrong. You trusted me and I treated that trust as if it was nothing. It was a cowardly, selfish, pathetic thing to do. I understand why it upset you and you were right to call me on it.'

She stared at him, her eyes wide with confusion. 'Okay. Well, thank you for apologising.'

'I destroyed that painting you saw, so you don't need to worry about it ever appearing.'

Releasing her arm and digging into his pocket, he pulled out a handful of long painted ribbons of canvas. 'This is all that's left of that painting and the one of you covered in paint.' He handed them to her and she stared down at them, her eyes widening in surprise.

When she looked back up into his face, her bottom lip was trembling and her eyes were shining with tears.

'What do you want me to say? That I'm pleased you tore your work apart?'

It was hell being this close to her without being allowed to enfold her in his arms and hold her close, to soothe all the pain away, but he knew he couldn't do that right now. The weight of his reputation for short, intense affairs with his muses lay heavily between them. He'd given her no reason to believe she was any different from the tens of women he'd already used up and cast aside.

'Let me show you what I replaced those pictures with,' he said, walking over to the light switches on the wall and flicking them up so the room was flooded with light.

He heard Jess gasp as she saw what he'd been pouring his heart into for the last month.

It took Jess a few moments for her eyes to adjust to the light before she could fully focus on what was in front of her.

There was a sculpture, made up of what looked like a multicoloured canvas stretched across a man-shaped frame, sitting in the middle of the room beneath four

white spotlights. His posture was tensed as if ready to
jump up and run forward, his hands gripping his knees,
but, eerily, there was a flat picture where the contours
of his face should be.

She walked towards it on shaking legs, utterly captivated, and as she peered closer she realised the flat
piece had a self-portrait of Xander's face painted on it,
showing an expression of such pain in his eyes it nearly
broke her heart to look at it. The word *loser* was painted
across his forehead in dark purple paint.

Dragging her gaze away from the face, she peered
more closely at the rest of the sculpture and realised
with a shock that the multicoloured body was made up
of hundreds of tiny paintings.

Of her.

In some of them she was smiling, some looking confused, some looking insecure. In fact, he seemed to have
captured every possible emotion she'd ever had in her
life. As if he *knew* her. As if he'd seen inside her and
understood exactly what made her tick.

There was something metallic and shiny protruding
from the chest of the sculpture, as if it had been dragged
out of his body and was hovering in mid-air before him.

Taking a deep, shuddering breath, she dropped to
her knees to study it more closely and realised it was a
small metal cage, in the shape of a heart with fine fili-
gree letters trapped inside it.

She peered closer, barely able to focus through a be-
wildering haze of emotions.

It was the word *Jess*.

It was Xander's own personal love letter to her.

She felt his footsteps behind her as they made the
stripped wooden floor bounce. Swivelling round, she
stood up and faced him, at a total loss for words.

He didn't say anything, just took her hand and gently led her out from under the spotlight into a room at the back of the gallery, motioning for her to sit down on a cream leather sofa set back against the wall.

She sat on the edge and watched him lower himself down next to her, her whole body shaking now. She had no idea how to deal with all this. After convincing herself she needed to put her fling with him down to a freak anomaly in the short history of her life, she'd never expected to see him again, let alone have to deal with something as surreal as having a piece of his art dedicated to her.

'Did…did I imagine the life-size naked model of you, made up of images of my face?' she asked, her voice faltering as she tried and failed to pull herself together.

He breathed out slowly, as if centring himself.

'I need to explain something to you.' He ran a hand over his face, then repositioned himself on the sofa so his body was twisted towards her. 'When I was younger my art was the thing that saved me from complete melt-down. I did it as an outlet for all the anger and shame I carried around with me. I never expected for a second I could make the sort of money I have from it. After years of being shoved into the category of *troublemaker* I was totally amazed when people began to talk about me in terms of having talent as an artist instead of just being a public nuisance with my "graffiti". Before I realised what was happening, my career began to gain this crazy momentum and I was suddenly propelled into the lime-light. People were interested in what I had to say, like it meant something important to them. It was a revelation. Instead of being a problem and a drain on the system, I was someone people wanted to be associated with.'

'And, boy, did you associate with them.' She gave him a tentatively playful smile, which he returned.

'Yeah, I know, I turned into a massive tart. Believe it or not, I was pretty freaked by all the attention to begin with. Suddenly women who wouldn't have given me the time of day before were throwing themselves at me left, right and centre. After the first few had been and gone and more were lining up right behind them, I went a bit wild with it. It felt like an opportunity to make up for all the lost time in my youth when everyone else had been out at parties and clubs and I'd been working my butt off just to keep myself alive.'

He ran a shaking hand through his hair and Jess had to force herself to let out the breath she'd been holding, her throat tight from trying not to cry.

'I was living the dream, until it all began to fall to pieces,' he continued. 'The critics got hold of me and tore my last exhibition to pieces, which wouldn't have been such a big deal on its own, but it was meant to be a slap in the face for my old man. Not that he ever got to see it. He died before I got to prove he was wrong about me being a waste of space and I've been carrying this rage around with me ever since. Until you turned up and helped me channel it into something positive.'

'Xander…I don't understand what you want from me. I thought you didn't *do* relationships?'

'I thought so, too, until I met you. I want to make this work between us, Jess. I want a real relationship with you, not some meaningless fling. You've made me re-evaluate everything I thought was important in my life. I don't want to be alone any more. I want to wake up in the morning and see that amazing smile of yours and know it's for me. That I've made you happy. That I'm worth more than my father told me I was.'

'You are. Oh, Xander, you are.'

'I laid myself bare for you. That's all of me, Jess.' He put a hand up to her face and stroked his fingers against her cheek, before sliding them into her hair and cupping the back of her head, drawing her mouth closer to his. 'After tonight the whole world's going to know how I feel about you.'

'I can't believe you did that. For me,' she murmured, the heat of his mouth driving her wild.

'Yeah, well, apparently being in love can make you do crazy things.'

'You love me?' The words came out as a gasp.

He smiled. 'Isn't it obvious? I didn't think I was capable of subtlety.'

Laughing, she pressed her mouth against his, basking in the familiar taste of him, the tantalising smell of his skin.

'I think you should move in with me,' he said, drawing back to look her in the eye.

'What?' she whispered.

He grinned. 'What's the matter, Miss Prim, too wild for you?'

She huffed out a laugh. 'I can handle wild. In fact I'm giving up on trying to control everything around me. I don't want to be sensible any more. I want fun and craziness. And to experience the ups and downs. With you.'

'It's going to be quite a ride, Jess,' he said, raising an eyebrow in challenge.

'Bring it on,' she said, leaning forward to plant a firm kiss on his lips.

The sound of the gallery door opening brought them

back to the present and Jess pulled away to look him in the eye. 'It sounds like your admirers are arriving.'

He looked at her with such sexual heat she thought she might melt into a puddle at his feet. 'They can wait,' he said, kicking the office door shut and enfolding her in his arms. 'Tonight is all about you, after all.'

* * * * *

Mills & Boon® Hardback

May 2014

ROMANCE

The Only Woman to Defy Him	Carol Marinelli
Secrets of a Ruthless Tycoon	Cathy Williams
Gambling with the Crown	Lynn Raye Harris
The Forbidden Touch of Sanguardo	Julia James
One Night to Risk it All	Maisey Yates
A Clash with Cannavaro	Elizabeth Power
The Truth About De Campo	Jennifer Hayward
Sheikh's Scandal	Lucy Monroe
Beach Bar Baby	Heidi Rice
Sex, Lies & Her Impossible Boss	Jennifer Rae
Lessons in Rule-Breaking	Christy McKellen
Twelve Hours of Temptation	Shoma Narayanan
Expecting the Prince's Baby	Rebecca Winters
The Millionaire's Homecoming	Cara Colter
The Heir of the Castle	Scarlet Wilson
Swept Away by the Tycoon	Barbara Wallace
Return of Dr Maguire	Judy Campbell
Heatherdale's Shy Nurse	Abigail Gordon

MEDICAL

200 Harley Street: The Proud Italian	Alison Roberts
200 Harley Street: American Surgeon in London	Lynne Marshall
A Mother's Secret	Scarlet Wilson
Saving His Little Miracle	Jennifer Taylor

Mills & Boon® Large Print
May 2014

ROMANCE

The Dimitrakos Proposition	Lynne Graham
His Temporary Mistress	Cathy Williams
A Man Without Mercy	Miranda Lee
The Flaw in His Diamond	Susan Stephens
Forged in the Desert Heat	Maisey Yates
The Tycoon's Delicious Distraction	Maggie Cox
A Deal with Benefits	Susanna Carr
Mr (Not Quite) Perfect	Jessica Hart
English Girl in New York	Scarlet Wilson
The Greek's Tiny Miracle	Rebecca Winters
The Final Falcon Says I Do	Lucy Gordon

HISTORICAL

From Ruin to Riches	Louise Allen
Protected by the Major	Anne Herries
Secrets of a Gentleman Escort	Bronwyn Scott
Unveiling Lady Clare	Carol Townend
A Marriage of Notoriety	Diane Gaston

MEDICAL

Gold Coast Angels: Bundle of Trouble	Fiona Lowe
Gold Coast Angels: How to Resist Temptation	Amy Andrews
Her Firefighter Under the Mistletoe	Scarlet Wilson
Snowbound with Dr Delectable	Susan Carlisle
Her Real Family Christmas	Kate Hardy
Christmas Eve Delivery	Connie Cox

0414 GEN STD LP

Mills & Boon® Hardback

June 2014

ROMANCE

Ravelli's Defiant Bride	Lynne Graham
When Da Silva Breaks the Rules	Abby Green
The Heartbreaker Prince	Kim Lawrence
The Man She Can't Forget	Maggie Cox
A Question of Honour	Kate Walker
What the Greek Can't Resist	Maya Blake
An Heir to Bind Them	Dani Collins
Playboy's Lesson	Melanie Milburne
Don't Tell the Wedding Planner	Aimee Carson
The Best Man for the Job	Lucy King
Falling for Her Rival	Jackie Braun
More than a Fling?	Joss Wood
Becoming the Prince's Wife	Rebecca Winters
Nine Months to Change His Life	Marion Lennox
Taming Her Italian Boss	Fiona Harper
Summer with the Millionaire	Jessica Gilmore
Back in Her Husband's Arms	Susanne Hampton
Wedding at Sunday Creek	Leah Martyn

MEDICAL

200 Harley Street: The Soldier Prince	Kate Hardy
200 Harley Street: The Enigmatic Surgeon	Annie Claydon
A Father for Her Baby	Sue MacKay
The Midwife's Son	Sue MacKay

Mills & Boon® Large Print

June 2014

ROMANCE

A Bargain with the Enemy	Carole Mortimer
A Secret Until Now	Kim Lawrence
Shamed in the Sands	Sharon Kendrick
Seduction Never Lies	Sara Craven
When Falcone's World Stops Turning	Abby Green
Securing the Greek's Legacy	Julia James
An Exquisite Challenge	Jennifer Hayward
Trouble on Her Doorstep	Nina Harrington
Heiress on the Run	Sophie Pembroke
The Summer They Never Forgot	Kandy Shepherd
Daring to Trust the Boss	Susan Meier

HISTORICAL

Portrait of a Scandal	Annie Burrows
Drawn to Lord Ravenscar	Anne Herries
Lady Beneath the Veil	Sarah Mallory
To Tempt a Viking	Michelle Willingham
Mistress Masquerade	Juliet Landon

MEDICAL

From Venice with Love	Alison Roberts
Christmas with Her Ex	Fiona McArthur
After the Christmas Party...	Janice Lynn
Her Mistletoe Wish	Lucy Clark
Date with a Surgeon Prince	Meredith Webber
Once Upon a Christmas Night...	Annie Claydon

Discover more romance at

www.millsandboon.co.uk

- ❤ WIN great prizes in our exclusive competitions

- ❤ BUY new titles before they hit the shops

- ❤ BROWSE new books and REVIEW your favourites

- ❤ SAVE on new books with the Mills & Boon® Bookclub™

- ❤ DISCOVER new authors

PLUS, to chat about your favourite reads, get the latest news and find special offers:

- Find us on facebook.com/millsandboon
- Follow us on twitter.com/millsandboonuk
- ❤ Sign up to our newsletter at millsandboon.co.uk